I0541050

Web of Conspiracy

Book One:
Death of a Hero

By

Herbert Grosshans

Published by
Mélange Books, LLC
White Bear Lake, MN 55110
www.melange-books.com

Web of Conspiracy, Book 1, Death of a Hero,
Herbert Grosshans, Copyright © 2011

ISBN: 978-1-61235-024-0

Names, characters, and incidents depicted in this book are products of the author's imagination or are used fictitiously. Any resemblance to actual events, locales, organizations, or persons, living or dead, is entirely coincidental and beyond the intent of the author or the publisher. No part of this book may be reproduced or transmitted in any form or by any means, electronic or mechanical, including photocopying, recording, or by any information storage and retrieval system, without permission in writing from the publisher.

Credits
Copy Edit; Sherry Der Wille
Line Edit: Nancy Schumacher
Format Editor: Mae Powers
Cover Artist: A.Bratt

Web of Conspiracy
Book One: Death of a Hero
By Herbert Grosshans

When Detective Jeff Chartrand investigates a grisly murder, his past catches up with him and flings him back into a world of violence he left behind years ago. He meets a mysterious woman who reveals a secret and he has an unexpected sexual encounter

Visit Herbert's website:
http://hegro.shawwebspace.ca
http://hegro.blogspot.com/

Works also by and including Herbert Grosshans:
Stars In Chains 1, Slave
Stars In Chains 2: Liberator
Stardogs 1 & 2
The Xandra Triology
Cliffs of Time
Orion the Hunt
Beyond the Stars Digest
Orion: Symbiont of Passion
Men of Eros

Chapter One

The thin material of the tent was the only protection from the fiery ball in the cloudless sky. It kept away the damaging rays but didn't do anything to keep out the blistering heat.

Jeff Chartrand stared at the shimmering mass of air hovering above the forever moving, forever shifting desert. The sand dunes looked like giant waves in a yellow sea, changing shape in slow motion as the hours passed. He watched the strong wind slowly creating a wall around the two tanks barely visible through the entrance of the tent, threatening to bury them under a thick blanket of sand.

In the distance, he could hear the sound of exploding shells as the Iraqi's fired their rocket launchers, searching for American positions. So far, none had come close enough to be of concern, but it was only a matter of time until one would find the camp.

"How long until those French will be here?"

Jeff looked over at Jerry Geisel and shrugged. "I have no idea. Ask the Lieutenant?"

"Another couple of hours. Maybe three." Lieutenant Bernard shifted in his seat by the entrance. His assault rifle lay within easy reach on the sandy ground. "Why?"

"I finished that stupid novel I was reading. What a bunch of crap! I don't know why these writers can't come up with better ideas. It's always the same. Lonely guy whose wife doesn't understand him meets beautiful, sexy girl."

"Why do you read that garbage in the first place?" Ray Tremmer asked with a sneer.

"Because I've got nothing else to read, idiot. I'm bored." Geisel gave the short and stocky Tremmer an angry stare.

4

Jeff glanced at Tremmer. A thin mustache, intended to make him look older, adorned his upper lip, but he still looked like a little boy to Jeff. He could never understand why a guy with a pronounced overbite would wear a mustache.

"So why don't you jerk yourself off to pass the time, idiot yourself." Tremmer stared back at Geisel, and then he grinned at Jeff.

Lieutenant Bernard gave him a stern look. "You know I don't like that kind of talk, Tremmer."

"Sorry, Lieutenant. I always forget you're a preacher."

The sarcasm in Tremmer's voice was obvious, but Bernard ignored it. "You watch for a while, Chartrand," he told Jeff. He looked at Tremmer. "By the way, I'm not a preacher, but I follow the teachings of our Lord. He is the reason I'm here in the first place."

"Forgive me. I thought you were here to protect the Saudis from Saddam Hussein and make sure we don't lose access to their precious oil wells. Now why would I think that?"

"Why indeed?" asked Jerry Geisel, grinning.

The sound of an explosion and shrapnel ripping through the thin fabric of the tent made Jeff hug the ground. He heard someone screaming. Looking around, he saw a fountain of crimson spraying out of Tremmer's shoulder where his arm should be. Beside him lay Lieutenant Bernard in a lifeless heap on top of Jesus Gomez. Or what was left of him.

Jeff registered all of this with clinical detachment. It didn't seem real. He became aware of more screaming and shouts outside, the sound of gunfire. Then nothing as the world sank into darkness.

"You'll be all right, buddy." The voice sounded far away. "Just hang in there."

He felt motion.

Opening his eyes, he looked into a woman's face. "What's your name, soldier?"

"Jeff. Jeffrey Chartrand." His voice came out in a whisper. There was pain in his belly and in his thigh.

"I need some help here," someone yelled. Then he felt the pressure of hands.

Darkness descended again, took away the pain.

* * * *

5

The sound of the alarm clock released him from his nightmare. Without looking at it, he hit it with his open hand, but it wouldn't stop.

"Damn!" he cursed and sat up, rubbing his eyes. Just once, I'd like to dream about something pleasant. How long will these images still torture me? It's been sixteen years.

Sighing, he threw back the covers and got out of bed. Then he pushed the button on the clock and looked at the display.

Six A.M. Saturday, March 17, 2007

"Nobody should have to get up this early," he mumbled to himself. Then he cursed again. This was Saturday. His day off. Shrugging, he went to the bathroom. Might as well stay up now. Looking into the mirror he said, "You're an idiot, Jeff Chartrand. Next time don't forget to shut off that damned alarm."

Today was his nephew's birthday. He had promised to be there.

* * * *

"Happy Birthday, Son."

Michael Chartrand lifted his glass in a toast.

Joseph looked at his father and smiled. "Thanks, Dad." He glanced at his sister Angie, grinning. "Dad told me he would let me drive that corvette he fixed up."

"You're only fourteen, you silly nut," Angie said. "You'll have to wait two more years until you get your driver's license."

"He can only drive it in the parking lot of our shop," Michael explained.

"Just be careful," Samantha Chartrand said, concern in her voice. She looked at her brother-in-law. "Jeffrey, you're Michael's older brother. Tell him it's not a good idea to put a fourteen year old behind the wheel of a sports car."

Jeff smiled at her and shrugged. "You may be talking to the wrong guy, Samantha. Michael and I, we already drove cars when we were twelve."

"On the farm," Samantha protested. "And those cars were old clunkers. They didn't go faster than ten miles an hour." She laughed. "If you were lucky."

"He's fourteen, for heaven's sake," Michael defended himself. "Almost a man."

6

"Sure. Next thing you'll tell him he should be looking for a wife." Samantha blew her husband a kiss across the table. Then she rose. "I'd better get the knife to cut the cake."

Jeff watched her walking into the kitchen. Looking at his brother, he said, "You're a lucky guy, Michael. You have a beautiful, great wife, a handsome son, and a lovely daughter."

"Thanks, big brother." Michael's face turned serious. "You should have married again, Jeff. How long are you going to mourn? It's been over ten years since Nicole passed away." He smiled. "You also have a beautiful daughter."

Jeff sighed. "She hardly knows I exist. She calls Barb Mom and Helmut Papa. I'm Jeff to her."

"She knows you're her real father. I'm sure deep down she loves you."

"Maybe I should have tried to raise her myself, instead of letting Barb talk me into having her live with them," Jeff mused.

"Don't beat yourself up over it. You know it wouldn't have worked," Michael said. "A cop living by himself, always working different shifts, never home. What kind of family life would Michelle have had? I would have done the same thing had I been in your shoes."

"How about blowing out those candles?" Samantha said as she walked back into the dining room.

"But don't spit on the cake," Angie told her brother. "Like last year."

"That's a lie! I never did."

"Okay, children, no arguing!" Samantha said sharply. She looked at Michael. "There's a call for you, Mike. Don't take too long, please."

"Who is it?"

Samantha shrugged. "Didn't say. Wanted to talk to you. He sounded...strange." She clapped her hands. "Okay, who wants a piece of cake?"

Jeff heard Michael's voice from the kitchen, but he couldn't make out any words. When Michael came back, he wore a serious expression on his face, but then he smiled, went to his son and shook his shoulders from behind. "All right, big guy, let's see how fast you can finish that piece of cake."

He sat down and attacked his own piece. When he reached for another one, Samantha slapped his hand. "Easy there, feller. Leave some for tomorrow. Your sister and the girls are coming for a visit."

"Yeah, tomorrow." Michael grinned lopsidedly. "Who knows what tomorrow brings." He stood up and put his arms around her. Kissing the top of her head, he said, "I love you all. Let's enjoy the day and being a family."

"Who was that on the phone?" Samantha asked.

"Nobody important." Michael shrugged it off. "Just an old army buddy. His name is Toby Miller."

"What did he want?"

"He wants to meet me. Talk about the old days, I guess."

"The old days?" Samantha laughed. "It's only been three years."

"Seems like only yesterday." Michael looked at his brother. "Doesn't it, Jeff?"

Jeff nodded, remembering his nightmares. "Sure does. Some things you never forget."

"No, you don't." Michael's eyes clouded over for a moment. "No matter how hard you try."

"Let's not go down that road again." Samantha shook her head, disapproval clearly showing in her face. "You men! I don't understand why you have to re-live it all over again. Isn't once enough?" Her eyes stabbed at her husband. "Nobody forced you to go a second time. I begged you not to."

"You did, didn't you?" Michael closed his eyes as if to shut out the world around him. "You'll never understand what it means to swear allegiance to the flag and to your country. You'll never understand what it means to be a soldier."

"You're right, Michael, I don't understand, and I will never understand why men have to kill each other. It is beyond my comprehension why you had to fight in this useless war. A war that is so wrong and should have never happened. How many American men and women still have to die trying to bring peace to a region that will never see peace? Those people don't think the way we do. They're all a bunch of religious zealots. How can you fight something like that?"

Samantha stopped to take a deep breath and looked around the suddenly silent table. Brushing her hand across her forehead, she smiled at her children. "Sorry, kids, I didn't mean to spoil the party. Sometimes I just get carried away. Why don't we all go into the living room and you can open the presents, Joey." She dabbed delicately at her eyes and wiped one finger across her cheeks.

Michael reached out to touch her hand. "That is all in the past, Sweetheart. Let's leave it at that, okay?"

She smiled bravely. "Okay. Sorry."

Michael looked at Jeff. "Want a beer? Helmut gave me some of that German stuff he always buys. He thinks our American beer is too weak."

Jeff laughed. "Sure, I'll have one. Good old Helmut. Doesn't like our cars, either. What can you do with a guy like that?"

"At least he's good with numbers. Saved me a few bucks last year on my income tax." Michael grinned. "Let's have a beer on our brother-in-law Helmut Helmann. Have you noticed? His accent is getting better."

Samantha chuckled. "You two, always making fun of him. He's not such a bad guy. He's trying. By the way, he doesn't like to be called 'Arnold'. Just thought I'll let you in on a little secret."

The brothers laughed.

"I think deep down Helmut wouldn't mind looking like our governor. He probably saw every movie he made when he was a movie star," Michael said. Then he went into the kitchen for the beer.

Jeff followed Samantha and the kids into the living room.

"I think you should talk to him in private some time," Samantha said with a low voice. "He's been depressed lately. Something's bugging him. He's trying to hide it, but I'm his wife. I know him. And that phone call? The same guy phoned yesterday. I recognized his voice." She looked up when Michael came back into the room and smiled at him. "How about me? Don't I deserve one of those German beers?"

"Sorry, Hon," Michael apologized. "I'll get you one."

Jeff took the offered bottle and sank into a chair. Maybe talking to his brother might do both of them good. There are some things you can only discuss with another man, some only with your brother.

"I will," he promised.

Chapter Two

It was a typical day in March. Slight drizzle and fog, with more to come the next few days…according to the weather forecast.

Jeff pulled up his collar and locked his car door. Nobody in his right mind would try to steal a car from a police parking lot, but these days anything was possible. Break-ins and robberies were up. Dozens of cars stolen every day. The courts wasted more time prosecuting these petty crimes than the more serious ones. Sometimes he didn't feel like even arresting a suspect, finding it a waste of time. Most of these criminals hired high-priced lawyers who didn't give a damn about justice. It was all about winning, never mind punishing the guilty.

He walked on, his head down, when a dark shadow crossed in front of him, almost making him stumble. He looked up to see a black cat scrambling over the fence. He smiled. Some people might read it as a bad omen.

"Hey, Jeff. Wait up."

He turned and waited for the tall blond woman to catch up with him. Maxine Montana, his partner.

"Had a good weekend?" she asked.

"Hi, Max." He gave her a friendly smile. "I did. Went to my nephew's birthday party. And you?"

"Spent the time cleaning out my fish tanks and listening to music. Bought a new CD by André Rieu." She glanced at him. "How's Michael doing?"

He shrugged. "Okay, I guess. He's got issues." He stopped and looked at her. "He and Darrin were good friends."

She seemed to have trouble with her eyes. "Yesterday it was three years," she said softly.

Jeff reached out to touch her shoulder. "I know. It's one of the dates I won't forget either. But always remember, your brother knew the risk, just like Michael, just like all of us."

"But Michael came back. Darrin didn't." She looked into the gray sky. "I hate March."

He grabbed her arm. "Let's get inside. I'll buy you a cup of coffee."

"Cheapskate." She grinned. "I'm not drinking that colored water Daniels brews for us. You can buy me lunch today. By the way, did you hear about that drive-by shooting up on Hillside Drive? Spencer is handling it. I hope he doesn't bungle it up again."

Captain Stoneman sat already behind his desk. Before Jeff had a chance to go to his own desk, the Captain motioned for him to come into his office.

"Tell Montana to join us," Stoneman told Jeff when he opened the door.

"Hey, Max," Jeff called to his partner. "Captain wants to see us."

"Anything wrong?" Montana asked when she stepped into the Captain's office.

"No." Stoneman shuffled some papers. "Well...yes. Call came in this morning. There's been an incident at 735 Riverdale Ave. One of the neighbors called it in. She sounded hysterical. The dispatcher couldn't understand much, except for the address and something about gunshots. Sheppard is already on his way, but I'd like you two to go and check it out."

"That's next to my brother's place," Jeff said slowly, letting out a breath of relief. "Two brothers live in that house with their mother. They've been in trouble with the law before. Wonder what they did this time?"

"You won't find out standing here." Stoneman waved his hand. "Go! Just don't do anything stupid." His eyes fixed on Jeff.

"I hear you, Chief," Jeff said. He turned to leave, winked at Montana.

She winked back and grinned. "I wonder what he's talking about," she mumbled under her breath.

"Same goes for you, Montana," the Captain called after them.

Traffic seemed unusually light, most likely because of the miserable weather, and it took just a little over half an hour to get to Riverdale Ave.

A patrol car was parked in front of the house with the number 735 boldly displayed above the door. Jeff parked his car behind it. Montana got out first and opened the gate to the house next to Michael's.

Jeff followed her slowly, instinctively loosening his gun in its holster. Before his partner reached the door, it opened and a young man with an unshaven face stuck out his head. "Can I help you?" he challenged them.

"Where is Detective Sheppard?" Montana asked.

The youth shrugged. "How the fuck should I know? You're the cop."

"Well, his car is parked in front of your house. He's got to be somewhere. Mind if we come in and have a look around?"

"Yes, I mind."

Montana put her hand on her gun but didn't draw it. "Move aside," she said her voice dangerously low.

"What the hell is going on?" asked a shrill voice from inside the house. A woman appeared in the doorway. Jeff recognized her as the young man's mother.

"Mrs. Burkhard, it's me, Jeff Chartrand, Michael's brother. One of your neighbors reported gunshots."

"Gunshots? Not in my house. This is so typical for you cops. My boys get into a little trouble just once, and every time something happens they are suspects."

An icy hand reached for Jeff's brain. He looked over to his brother's house, a terrible knot suddenly in his stomach.

"I'd like to come in anyway and check things out."

He heard Montana speak, but he didn't pay much attention. The door to Michael's house opened and the familiar figure of Detective Sheppard stepped onto the concrete platform. He turned his head and looked at Jeff. "You've got the wrong house," Sheppard called.

Jeff didn't bother to walk back on the sidewalk. He crossed the yard and jumped over the three-foot fence.

Sheppard's face looked gray. "Better take a deep breath before you go in there," he said.

Jeff brushed him aside, almost ran into the house. A loud moan of anguish escaped his lips when he saw Samantha's lifeless body sprawled on the living room floor. Her white nightgown was stained red, one of her breasts exposed where someone had ripped the gown.

Michael sat on the couch. He looked straight ahead, his eyes open, unseeing, like a man in deep thought. A small round hole in his forehead belied that impression. The dark material of the couch seemed a little darker where he sat. On the table in front of him, lay a package. It looked like a small pillow. From a cut on one side, white powder spilled onto the dark wood of the shiny tabletop, shimmering like tiny ice crystals on the surface of a huge bowl filled with tar.

"Looks like a drug deal gone wrong. That's a hell of a lot of cocaine," Sheppard said behind him.

Jeff turned around, fists lifted in anger, ready to strike out at anything and anyone.

"Take it easy, Jeff." Montana stood in the doorway, a look of shock and pity on her face. She strode into the room and looked at the overturned furniture, the ripped-open drawers. "Whoever did this clearly looked for something, but nothing seems to be missing. Nothing obvious, anyway." She looked at Jeff. "Call it in and ask the Captain to send someone else."

Jeff shook his head. "No. I need to know what happened. I need to find out first hand." He had trouble formulating the words. His mind seemed to be frozen in a sea of ice. He moved like a man in a dream. Everything seemed to slow down and Sheppard's and Montana's voices sounded hollow and far away. He bounded up the stairs, taking three at a time. His fears were confirmed when he saw the open door to Joseph's room.

Joseph lay on his bed, still covered with his blanket. Only his head was visible. He lay on his back, his eyes closed. The blue blanket showed a dark stain.

The door to Angie's room was closed. When he saw the curled-up body on top of the bed and the pool of red on the white linen, he let out a cry of despair. Three steps took him to the bed. Against his better judgment, he touched her small body. Then he noticed the long blond hair.

Angie had black hair.

Realizing it wasn't Angie, he looked into the girl's face. He didn't recognize her. She appeared to be about the same age as Joseph. He turned to see Montana walking into the room. "That's not my niece," he said, his voice dead, without emotion. "Did you find another body?"

"No, only two adults." She hesitated. "Your brother and his wife." She looked around. "Nothing seems to be disturbed in this room," she commented. Stepping up to the bed, she studied the girl. "Who is she?"

Jeff shrugged. "Probably Joseph's study partner. I don't know her. Where is Angie?"

"Not in the house."

Jeff examined the girl's body, his jaws clenched. "She was shot at close range, just like Joseph. In her sleep. Who could do something like this? She's no older than fourteen. A child."

"Have you touched anything, Jeff?" Montana asked.

"Just the girl. On the shoulder."

"Good. The forensic team will want to go over the entire scene. In the meantime, we should talk to the neighbors. Maybe somebody saw something."

"How about the woman who phoned it in?" Jeff brushed his eyes. His chest ached, he was aware of his beating heart and he seemed to have trouble breathing.

This was not the first time he'd seen dead people, but this was different. This was his brother. Family. "Fuck it!" he cursed loudly and hit the doorframe with his flat hand. "I will find the ones who did this, I promise. They'll pay for this!" His jaw and teeth hurt as he ground them and his words came out distorted, like sounds from the throat of a wild beast.

He followed Montana slowly down the stairs. Nothing had changed in the living room. Michael still sat on the couch, his open eyes staring straight ahead, giving the impression of a man lost in a daydream.

Jeff expected him to snap out of it at any moment and offer him a beer. His eyes fell on Samantha, at her exposed breast. Someone should cover her up. Nobody needs to see her like this. It's degrading. However, he knew there was nothing he could do. He might disturb important evidence. When he heard a cell phone ringing, it took him a moment to realize it was his own.

"Chartrand?"

"Yes, Captain?" He spoke harshly, angry to be interrupted in his contemplation.

14

"I just finished talking to Sheppard. Sorry about your brother. I'm taking you off the case." Captain Stoneman sounded impartial, without emotion, but Jeff knew different.

The Captain lost his son years earlier. While making an arrest, he was shot point blank in the face by the driver of a stolen vehicle. He died instantly. The Captain took off a year of absence after the murder. Many in the department didn't believe he would come back, but he did, and he recovered from the terrible loss.

Hearing the Captain's voice brought back a measure of sense to Jeff. "I understand, Captain, but I wish you'd reconsider." He forced himself to stay calm. "I can handle it."

"This is not up for discussion, Chartrand. Take the rest of the day off. Come into my office before you go home. Tell Montana to hitch a ride with Sheppard."

"Yes, sir," Jeff said, resigning to the fact it was useless to argue.

His partner gave him an inquiring look. "Stoneman?" she asked.

Jeff nodded. "You're supposed to hitch a ride with Sheppard."

"It's better this way, Jeff. You could not stay impartial." Montana shook her head when she looked at Samantha's bloody form on the floor. "We'll get the son of a bitch who did this. I won't let him get away."

Jeff stared at the package on the table, at the white powder on the dark surface. "Michael never did drugs and he didn't deal. I know my brother."

Detective Sheppard came out of the study in the back. He carried an attaché case. "I found this under the desk, hidden behind the computer." He opened it and let Jeff see the contents. "There's about twenty grand in there, I figure."

"My brother didn't have that kind of money," Jeff said stubbornly. "This looks more and more like a setup to me."

"You're off the case, Chartrand." Sheppard said. "Let me handle this."

Jeff glared at him. He never liked the short detective. "I'm warning you, Sheppard. Don't blow this one! I'll be watching." With one last look at his dead brother, he left the house, his thoughts in turmoil, his mind numb, unable to think coherently.

I'll have to tell Mom and Dad and I don't know how.

And Barb.

He choked back a sob and threw a glance at Mrs. Burkhard's house.

Wonder if those boys had something to do with it? At least one of them is dealing in drugs, I'm sure of it.

"Detective?"

He turned to look at the woman who stood in front of the house across the street.

"I'm the one who called the station," she said. "Is everything all right in there?"

Jeff hesitated. "No," he said. "There has been a shooting." He walked up to her.

The woman looked at him. Her eyes widened as she recognized him. "You're Michael's brother, Jeff," she said.

He nodded, not remembering her name for a moment, but then her name popped into his head. "What did you see or hear, Mrs. Sanderson?"

"I heard shots. Late last night. I couldn't sleep, so I got up to get a drink. I looked at the clock. It was five minutes to one. That's when I heard the gunshots. Two of them."

"How did you know they were gunshots?"

She smiled. "I watch a lot of television. Besides, I used to go target shooting when my husband was still alive. I can tell the difference between gunshots and the sound of a car backfiring."

"You're sure you only heard two?"

"I'm sure."

They must have used silencers with the kids. This was cold-blooded and deliberate murder. "Did you see anything else?" he asked.

"A car. It was dark and the lighting is bad on our street. It was also cloudy. I couldn't really see much. Two guys got into the car. One was big, the other just a regular guy. Couldn't make out their faces." She smiled again. "I ran to get my binoculars, but when I came back to the window the car was gone. Sorry."

"You've been a great help, Mrs. Sanderson," Jeff said.

"Call me Edith."

"Thanks, Edith. Did you report it right away?"

"No, not right away. I didn't know if I should get involved." She shrugged. "I've seen too many crime shows. I was scared, but then I got to thinking. Samantha and Michael, they were always nice to me.

Always friendly and saying hi. Michael fixed my fence once." She squinted when she looked at Jeff. "Did anyone get hurt?"

"I'm afraid so, Edith." Jeff swallowed a few times, seeing the picture of Michael on the couch with a hole in his head; Samantha on the floor; Joseph and the girl in their beds, their covers bloodstained. He had trouble getting out the words, but when he finally managed to speak, his voice came out in a hoarse whisper, "This is unofficial, but they're all dead."

Mrs. Sanderson put her hands over her mouth. "All of them?" she gasped. "Even the kids?"

Jeff nodded. "Yes, even the kids." He didn't mention that Angie wasn't among the slain, and that the dead girl was someone else. "I'd appreciate it if you kept it to yourself for now. And don't tell anyone you heard it from me, please."

"Oh, I won't, Jeff. Not a word. This is terrible." Her eyes filled with tears. "They were such beautiful and well-behaved children, always so polite. Who would do such a thing and why?"

"I don't know, Edith, but we'll find out." Jeff turned away and headed for his car.

Captain Stoneman waited for him in his office.

"I'm asking for one favor, Chief. Can we keep this under wraps until tomorrow? I don't want my sister and parents finding out on the six o'clock news."

"I'll try, Jeff, but you know how it is. This kind of thing always leaks out."

Jeff phoned Barbara to see if she was home, and then he took one of the longest drives he ever had to take.

Chapter Three

It was lunchtime when he drove into the driveway of his sister's house. Barbara was busy making lunch for the girls who'd be coming home from school. As much as he looked forward to seeing his daughter, that's how much he dreaded this visit.

"Hi, Jeff," Barbara said cheerfully when he walked into the house. "What brings you here?"

When she saw his solemn expression, she stared at him, knowing immediately something was wrong. "What is it? Something happened to Mom and Dad?"

"No." He stepped up to her and took her into his arms.

"What is it, Jeff?" she asked again. "Tell me."

He felt her tremble in his arms. "It's Michael," he finally said, his voice choked with emotion. "Last night. There has been a shooting."

"Oh, my god! Michael's been shot. How? What happened? How bad is it?" She stepped out of his embrace and stared at him, her eyes wide. He knew that she was afraid to ask the next question, afraid of what she would hear. When he stayed silent, she cried out, "No, no. Not Michael! Is he...?" She didn't finish the sentence.

He nodded, unable to speak for a moment. Somehow, his throat refused to say what he had to tell her next.

Barbara's face had taken on the color of chalk, but the tears didn't come...not yet.

He forced himself to speak. "Michael, Samantha, and Joseph. They're all dead."

The words hung in the air, frozen in time. He heard them over and over in his head as he looked into Barbara's tormented face.

"No, no..." Her anguished cry tore through him, awakening memories he had tried so hard to forget.

18

Oh, Nicole. Why did you have to drive that night during the thunderstorm?

"Tell me it's not true. Please, Jeffrey…"

He pulled her into his arms again, held her, afraid to let her go, for fear she might disappear like everyone else he loved. "I wish I could," he whispered, "but I can't."

Her tears burst out of her.

"Angie wasn't there," he said. "I don't know what happened to her."

"She spent the night here, with us," Barbara sobbed. "I drove her to school this morning. Can you pick her up? I don't know if I can drive."

"I took the day off," Jeff said. Then he went to sit in one of the kitchen chairs to take the weight off his suddenly weak legs.

"How did it happen?"

"We don't know. The detective in charge suggested it was drugs." He lifted a hand when Barbara opened her mouth in protest. "I told him he's wrong, but they found a package with some stuff that looked liked cocaine on the table in front of Michael. And a large sum of money under his desk. It doesn't look good."

"You're a homicide detective, Jeff. Why aren't you handling the case?"

"My captain took me off the case."

"Why? You're the best."

He smiled thinly. "I wish everyone in the precinct would think that. Life would be a lot easier." He looked at the picture of three young people on one of the kitchen walls. Two boys, ages fourteen and nine. Between them a big-eyed girl with black wild hair, age six. He smiled. Barb's hair still looked like that most of the time.

His brother's blue eyes stared at him out of a freckled face. Michael was the only one in the family with blue eyes, inherited from his great-grandmother.

Jeff looked at himself in the picture. Even at fourteen, he had been big for a boy his age. Black hair, spiked in the middle, and the brown eyes of his grandmother, who had been a full-blooded Sioux.

"Why aren't you handling it?" Barbara broke into his thoughts.

"Rules. I might harbor thoughts of revenge and do something that would carry dire consequences."

"That is a stupid rule. They should put their best investigator on this." Barbara broke into tears again. "It doesn't seem real," she moaned. "At any moment I expect to wake up from this nightmare. Poor Angie. What's going to happen to her? She'll have to live with us. She can have the spare room in the basement. Or maybe I should put Mandy and Michelle into one room. They're the same age, and Angie can have Michelle's room."

Sobbing, she sat down. "My knees are all wobbly," she said, trying to smile.

"Why don't you phone Helmut and ask him to come home," Jeff suggested.

"Oh, god, oh god, we'll have to arrange a funeral. Three caskets."

He reached across the table and patted her hand. "One thing at a time, sis. By the way, there was someone else. A girl. She was about Joseph's age. Blond hair. I didn't recognize her."

"She's dead too?" Barbara asked, shocked.

"They probably thought it was Angie. Do you have an idea who she was?"

"Nellie Keller. She is one of Joseph's friends from school. They study together. She helps him with geography." She covered her face with her hands. "Her parents will be devastated. She's their only child." She stared a Jeff. "I don't want them to sweep this under the table. Or make it sound as if Michael is the guilty one. Promise me that, Jeff."

"I promise," Jeff said grimly. "I may be off the case, officially, but I will not rest until the guilty are found and punished."

He stayed with his sister until it was time to pick up Angie. When he left, Helmut hadn't come home yet; neither had Mandy and Michelle.

Angie was surprised to see him. "Hi, Uncle Jeff. How come you're picking me up? Anything wrong with Aunt Barbara?"

"No, nothing is wrong with your aunt, but…" he started and paused when his throat refused to say more. Swallowing hard, he said, "I have some awful news about your mom and dad…" He stopped again, unable to carry on. How do you tell a child her parents have been murdered? By the way, your parents are dead, but don't worry, everything is going to be okay.

Her eyes hung on his face, waiting for him to tell her. "What about my mom and dad?" she asked in a small voice.

He touched her cheek with a gentle gesture. "I don't know how to tell you, Sweetheart, but some bad people did something bad to your mom and dad and to Joseph..."

She didn't reply, only looked at him with her large eyes. "Something bad?" she finally asked.

He nodded. "Yes. Something really bad." He fought back tears. He needed to be strong for her so she could be strong. He took her small hands into his. "Your parents and your brother...are in heaven now," he said with a choked voice, not sure how he could put it into the right words. They are in heaven... Where is heaven?

"Are they dead?"

Looking into her eyes, he couldn't speak, only nod.

"Yes, Joseph too."

"Not Joseph. He's my only brother. Oh please tell me this is just a game you're playing. Please." Her eyes filled with tears and a sob escaped her lips. Then she screamed, dropped her backpack, and threw herself against him. Her little body was racked by loud sobs as she clung to him.

He cursed the people who did this to her, cursed the god who let it happen. She was only a little girl. Bad things shouldn't happen to little girls.

"What am I going to do now, Uncle Jeff? I have no parents, no brother. Nobody. I'm all alone," she sobbed.

"You're not alone. You can stay with Aunt Barbara. She said to tell you that. She also said she will take good care of you. I promise you'll never be alone. We are here for you." Words. You can say so much with words...and so little.

She let go of him and stood with her arms hanging from her thin shoulders. She looked so frail, so vulnerable, and scared. He bent down to pick up her backpack and reached for her hand. "Come on, Sweetheart," he said gently. She walked beside him like a zombie, her eyes staring straight ahead, empty of expression and glazed over with tears. He opened the door of the car for her, and she slumped into the seat.

She didn't object when he fastened her seatbelt, just sat there, staring out of the window. Once in a while a loud sob shook her little body.

He drove on in silence, searching unsuccessfully for something comforting to say. It was difficult for him to deal with the fact his brother, his sister-in-law, and his nephew had been murdered. How could he expect an eleven year old child to deal with it rationally?

"I guess I'll be staying with Uncle Helmut and Aunt Barbara now forever," she said after awhile, breaking the silence.

"As long as you want to," he told her.

"It won't be so bad," she said with a calmness he knew she didn't feel. It would take a long time for her to really understand and realize she was the only survivor of her immediate family. Time would help her to adjust, but for now she was scared, afraid of the future.

So was Jeff but for different reasons. What would happen if whoever did this found out Angie was still alive? What if they tried to finish the job? His sister and her family, including his own daughter Michelle, could be in danger.

There was an urgency to find the killers and eliminate the threat.

Helmut was there when he got back to his sister's place. He showed great sympathy, even though he sometimes conveyed the impression of being cold and uncaring. "Angie can live with us. I have no problem with that. She is my family too, you know." He gave Jeff an awkward hug and clapped him on the back. "Sorry for your loss. Michael was a good guy. Always full of jokes. I'll miss him."

Jeff spent the evening with them. Then he drove home. He tried to phone Montana, but when she didn't answer her cell, he left a message with her answering service.

Sleep didn't come easy that night. When he slept, he kept seeing Michael sitting on the couch, a small hole in his forehead. Michael put his finger into the hole, and then he pulled it out, bloody, held it high into the air, while he gave Jeff an accusing stare. Samantha rose from the floor where she lay and began dancing, her bloodstained nightgown swirling around her slender form.

Suddenly, there was another woman in the room. She smiled through the film of dried blood that covered her face. "Dance with me, my Darling," she said to Jeff, her arms reaching for him.

Nicole.

As he moved toward her, the flesh melted from her bones and he stepped into the open arms of a skeleton.

"Dance, my Darling, dance." Her grinning, white skull bopped up and down, her jaws moved as she spoke, and her laughter echoed through the room.

Jeff awoke, slick with perspiration.

Five A.M.

Since he couldn't sleep anymore after that, he dressed, washed, and made himself a cup of coffee. Suddenly he felt like having a cigarette, but he gave up that habit in 1991, after coming back from Kuwait. Cigarettes were cheap in the army and gave you something to do when lying in the hot sand of the desert, waiting. As a civilian, he found smoking a filthy habit and too expensive to maintain.

He left for work at seven o'clock.

Captain Stoneman called him into his office the moment he sat down at his desk. "There is going to be a press conference this morning. We'll release as little as possible."

"Does that mean you've found something?"

Stoneman shrugged. "Truthfully? No. And if we had something, I'm sorry, Jeff, but you won't have access to that information." He gave Jeff a long look. "I won't have you acting on suspicions. We'll get the bastards, but it'll be done by the book, you understand?"

"I understand."

"I hope you do. Sheppard will head the investigation. I'm assigning Montana as his temporary partner. Until further notice." He paused. "You'll be working narcotics for a while. I spoke with Lieutenant Beacher. He's more than happy to have you."

Jeff nodded slowly. Beacher and he had been rookie cops together. He was an amiable guy. "When will I be transferred?"

"Tomorrow. Clean out your desk. Anything you're working on, give it to Detective Montana." He smiled. "If something develops, I'll keep you informed."

Montana was at her desk when Jeff walked out of the Captain's office. "He's transferred me to narcotics," he told her.

"You should have no problem there," she commented. "You've worked narcotics before." Looking at one of her files, she said with a hushed voice only he could hear, "Meet me for coffee at Rembrandt's. Ten o'clock. There's something I need to tell you."

She waited for him already when he got there.

"I wish someone else would handle it but Sheppard. He's an overzealous son of a bitch," she said when he sat down. "I'm not supposed to be talking to you. They found empty needles in your brother's house. The medical examiner will be testing the bodies for drugs."

Jeff sat there, his face a mask, his jaws working. "I know my brother. He never did drugs. Not as a civilian and not during his years in the army. And he never dealt. This is a setup. It's so plain, it's almost laughable."

"You're saying someone is going that much out of his way to frame your brother? There was a fortune there in drugs alone, never mind the twenty thousand in cash Sheppard found. Why would anyone do that?"

"To lead us away from the truth, what else? They're laying a false trail."

"An expensive trail. Maybe you didn't know your brother as well as you think, Jeff?"

"Fuck it!" he cursed. "Not you too, Max. I was counting on you being impartial."

"I am, Jeff. That's why I'm on the case and not you. You could never be impartial."

"Anything else you found out? Something useful, perhaps?"

"Did you know your brother may have had connections to the mob?"

"Michael? Never!" He spoke with a loud, angry voice, causing other patrons in the restaurant to look his way.

"Well, we found the business card of one Joseph Galliano in your brother's desk. Galliano is a well-known mobster. Maybe your brother crossed him and Galliano put out a contract on him. It's a lead and we have to follow it." Montana studied Jeff's face. "Did your brother ever mention Galliano or give you hints that he might have gotten over his head with something?"

"Not that I can recall. Michael was a mechanic. He fixed cars. At work and as a hobby. He was also an army lieutenant. He received a medal of valor, for God's sake. He was a good soldier and an upstanding citizen, not a criminal!" Jeff said vehemently.

"He was in Iraq. An ugly place. It could have changed him."

"That was his second tour of duty. He also served in Bosnia."

24

"That's what I mean. Maybe fighting in two wars was too much for him. Perhaps he became discouraged, started doing drugs. It happened. I know a lot of people who don't support the war in Iraq. Maybe he figured society owes him." She shrugged. "I don't know. Did he see a shrink after he came back?"

"Many soldiers do. I did. It means nothing. As you said, Iraq is an ugly place to be right now. War is ugly. It screws up your mind and when you come back to civilian life you have to adjust. That doesn't mean you'll turn into an addict or become a criminal."

"He was there when Darrin was killed. Did he ever talk to you about it?"

"A couple of times, but he never told me any details. He didn't like talking about his time over there. None of us do."

"You ever get the impression he was hiding something?"

"Something was bothering him," he admitted. "I don't know if it had anything to do with your brother's death."

Montana got up. "I'd better be going. Got to keep an eye on Sheppard. I'm sure he's keeping an eye on me." She chuckled. "For different reasons, though."

Jeff watched her walk away. Blond, blue-eyed, at five foot eight she presented an imposing figure of a woman. Beautiful, too. And not to be underestimated. Most men seem to underestimate beautiful women. She had a black belt in martial arts and beat most male cops at the shooting range.

Besides being a good cop, she was also trustworthy and a loyal partner. He knew she'd keep him informed. Mulling over what she'd told him, doubts began to sneak into his mind. Could he have been so wrong about Michael? His own brother?

Of one thing he was certain. Michael never dealt in drugs.

Never!

Had he used? Jeff suddenly didn't know anymore what to think. He needed to get his hands on the medical examiner's report. It shouldn't be difficult to find out if his brother had been a longtime user. He could almost accept it with Michael but not with Samantha. She was way too levelheaded for that.

Had been.

Jeff swallowed down that sudden lump in his throat. Damn! He couldn't just sit here and do nothing. Barbara would be making the funeral arrangements, but they couldn't really do much until the medical examiner's office released the bodies.

Why would Michael have Joseph Galliano's business card in his desk?

There was only one way to find out. He'd have to pay Galliano a visit.

Unofficially.

He might even be able to lean on him a little, officially, since he'd be working narcotics.

Chapter Four

They tried to keep the funeral as private as possible, but you can't bury a war hero without attracting attention, especially when the papers reported it with headlines like Was local war hero murdered by drug dealers?

Jeff was furious when he read those headlines and wowed to have a talk with the reporter and the editor of the paper. And with Stoneman. Someone in the department leaked classified information.

Funerals are at best sad occasions, but when you bury a loved-one, in this case three, it is not easy to be objective. Even so, Jeff managed to look around the assembled mourners. Most of them were relatives, friends, and neighbors. All of Michael's co-workers were there, some of them with their families.

Michael had been a popular guy.

He didn't miss the black sedan parked on one of the gravel roads inside the cemetery. No one got out, and the car took off before the coffins were lowered into the ground. Unfortunately, the car was not close enough to get a license plate number. He didn't mention the car to anyone, especially not to Barbara. No need to burden her with more worries.

Whoever it was, assuming they had anything to do with the murders, knew now that there had been only three coffins.

After the funeral and the reception in the funeral hall, the family went to Barbara's house. Samantha's brother, Frank, who lived in Boston, and her two sisters, Evelyn and Shawna, both of them from Denver, were also present.

Evelyn, short and petite, seemed to be the most affected. She was the youngest and had only been eleven when Samantha married Michael and moved away. "I didn't really know my sister." Sobbing, she looked at Jeff with her dark, large eyes, now red and swollen from crying. "She was a good person, wasn't she? I read the papers about the drugs. Is that true?"

"They're lies. Speculation. Don't you believe a word of it."

Shawna wasn't married, and he found her quite attractive. Doing a quick calculation in his head, he concluded she was twenty-six years old. Samantha had been thirty-three. She married Michael at age eighteen. He wondered why Shawna was still single. As good-looking as she was, she shouldn't have any trouble finding a guy. Unless she didn't swing that way.

This was the first time Jeff saw her. He knew nothing about her. Maybe she likes women more than men.

"We hardly visited," Shawna interrupted his thoughts. "I feel so bad about it." She broke into tears again. "Last time I saw my nephew Joseph, he was eight years old. That was six years ago," she sobbed. "How can families stay apart for so long? And now they're all gone."

"It's been over a week since the murders. Why haven't they found the guilty ones yet?" a man said behind Jeff.

Jeff turned and looked at the speaker. A man in his early sixties, judging by his nearly white hair and gray, small goatee.

Samantha's father.

"Progress is being made, Professor Bailey," Jeff told him. "These investigations take time."

"Pah. The police are doing nothing. As usual. The more time passes, the better the chances of the murderers getting away with it. And if they are found, some smart-ass, fast-talking lawyer will get them off. And the judges aren't much better. They hardly hand out sentences that fit the crime." He glared at Jeff from under bushy eyebrows. "You're a cop. You know how these things work. It's all politics."

"Calm down, Bill, please. Think of your ulcers." The woman beside him put her hand on his arm. She turned to Jeff. "Don't take him seriously. He has all these conspiracy theories in his head. He doesn't mean to offend you."

Jeff smiled at her. "I'm not offended, Mrs. Bailey."

"Mary. Call me Mary." She smiled. "Mrs. Bailey sounds so official."

"I only speak the truth," Professor Bailey said gruffly. "What have the police found out, if anything?"

Jeff lifted his shoulders in a defensive gesture. "I am not on the case."

"Why not?" Bailey asked with a belligerent voice.

"Because I am Michael's brother."

"As I said. Politics."

"Not politics. Policy. Rules. Believe me, Professor, I wish I were on this case. I'm as anxious as anyone else to find the murderers and punish them."

The professor snorted in disgust. "Punish them? How? By sending them to jail where they get three meals a day, watch TV, get educated, play sports… It's like a holiday. And then some lawyer who doesn't care about justice, only about winning another case, maybe become famous, gets them out in three years. There's your punishment for you."

"Is my father putting down the lawyers again?" The tall man with the small mustache smiled at Jeff. "I'm Frank Bailey, Samantha's brother. I don't know if you remember me. The last time we spoke was at my sister's wedding."

Jeff shook the outstretched hand. "I remember our talk. We argued about America's involvement in the Gulf war. You're the attorney."

"I still don't believe we should have gotten involved. In the gulf war and now in Iraq. This war is so wrong. We should have left Saddam Hussein alone. At least he ruled with an iron fist, kept these religious nuts under control. Sure, he killed a few people, but more people have died in this war than he ever killed. And more are dying every day. It will be a long time before there is peace in that region, if ever. Besides, Iraq never had those weapons of mass destruction, but we have them. I guess that's all right, because we're the good guys."

Jeff gave him a thin smile. "You have the right to your opinion, but many Americans think differently. We're fighting for the freedom not only for our country but also for the rest of the world. We're trying to protect our way of life. Your way of life, Frank."

"But at what cost? Did you hear Senator Osborne the other day? He suggested we invade Iran. He reasons that Iran poses a threat to world peace because it possesses nuclear reactors and possibly nuclear weapons. The Israelis say they don't have nuclear weapons. Can we believe them? Even if they had, I guess, it would be all right because they are on our side. How about North Korea? Should we invade them also?"

"Nobody suggests that, Frank."

"No? I'll tell you why. They have no oil. Everything is about oil." Frank stared at Jeff. "A few days ago I saw an interview with retired General Mathew Parker. He thinks we should increase our presence in Afghanistan. And Senator Osborne backs him up. The Taliban are getting stronger every day, he said. According to him, the Canadians aren't doing enough. Meanwhile, they're fighting a war they weren't even supposed to fight. Their role in Afghanistan has been stepped up from peacekeeping to active involvement, while the other members of NATO are doing nothing to help them. The Canadians are losing a lot of young men in that war."

"People die in war. That's a sad fact," Jeff said, irritated by Frank's insinuations.

"Men!" Mary Bailey said exasperated. "Always talking politics. Are there no other topics you can discuss?"

"Sure, Mother. We could talk about golf," Frank said.

"I'm afraid not me." Jeff shook his head. "I don't play golf. That's for old men as far as I'm concerned."

"What do you play?"

"I used to play football in college. I was actually pretty good, but now I box in the little spare time I have."

"I don't like boxing," Mary said. "I think it's barbaric. Two grown men beating each other bloody until one lies unconscious."

Jeff smiled. "It doesn't need to go that far. By the way, many women also box," he said, remembering Nicole. With her long legs, she had taken up kickboxing and she had been darn good at it. Never once did she get kicked in the face. It would have been a shame to ruin that pretty face of hers.

"I think I could get interested in that." Frank grinned. "I mean, watching two scantily dressed women going at each other..."

"Do we really need to discuss this?" Shawna asked. "We just buried Samantha and her family. Let's show some respect, please."

"There is Angie," Mary said. "I haven't seen her since Christmas a year ago. How she's grown." She dabbed her eyes. "Excuse me. I'm going to talk to my granddaughter. She must feel terribly alone right now." She walked away.

Shawna looked after her and shook her head. "My mother. I'm surprised she remembered Angie's name."

"You're giving her too little credit, sis," Frank said.

"Well, you always take her side."

Jeff turned away, having found an excuse to leave. He went into the kitchen for a drink. Michelle stood in front of an open cupboard. "Hi, Jeff." She gave him a bright smile.

"Hi, Michelle." Jeff stroked her hair. "You look cute in braids." He wanted to take her into his arms and hug her close to him, wanted to tell her how much he loved her and please, call me Dad. She was only eleven, but he had missed the time for that by a few years. He would never be Dad to her, just Jeff.

"How's school?" he asked.

"Fine." She looked up at him. "Angie's been crying a lot these past few days. She misses her mom and dad, and she wants to go to her house. All her stuff is there. When can she go home?"

"I don't know. That's up to the investigators. They're still searching the house for evidence."

"What's evidence?"

"They're hoping to find some clues that may lead them to the people who did this terrible thing to Uncle Mike, Aunt Samantha, and to Joseph."

"Is Angie going to stay here forever now?"

Jeff smiled. "Not forever, I hope, but until she's grown."

Michelle screwed up her face. "I guess she'll have to change schools. I mean, the one she's going to now is too far from here." She looked thoughtful. "Will she call my parents Mom and Papa, like me, after my real mom died and you gave me up?"

Startled, Jeff stared at her, the implication of what she said hitting him hard. He crouched in front of her and took her small face between his hands. "You were a baby when your mother died, and I didn't know what to do. Your...mom, my sister, offered to raise you. I thought it best for both of us. I never gave you up, Sweetheart. You're still my daughter and I love you."

He tried to suppress it, but his eyes suddenly filled with tears. Letting go of her face, he rose and swallowed the hard lump in his throat. "Were you looking for something special in the cupboard?" he asked with a croaky voice.

She didn't seem to notice his inner turmoil. "Tacos," she said.

He found the bag and pulled it out of the cupboard. "This one?"

She took it. "Thanks, Jeff." Then she whirled and skipped away.

"She's full of spunk and a joy to have around."

Jeff turned to look at Barbara, who stood in the doorway, smiling. "She reminds me a lot of Nicole when she was her age."

"I guess you'd remember that more than I," Jeff said. "You and Nicole were good friends when you were little girls. I didn't notice her until my hormones started to interfere with my brain." He smiled. "How are you holding up?"

"Hanging in there, I guess. It'll take some adjusting having another girl around, but we'll be fine. Helmut gives me a lot of support."

"He's a great guy, even though he's German." Jeff chuckled, unable to refrain from making a little teasing joke about his brother-in-law. "Not many men would agree to raise someone else's children."

She smiled a little, knowing that Jeff didn't mean anything by his remark; except that it was his way of saying he was fond of Helmut. "You're right, he is a great guy, and he's also a good father." She came into the kitchen and stood in front of him. "Have they found any new leads?"

Shaking his head, he said, "I haven't spoken to Maxine, but they're shutting me out. I might know more by tomorrow." He hesitated, not sure if he should tell her. "I saw a car today. At the funeral. I find it odd, that's all. It may mean nothing, but we can't ignore it. I want you to be careful and alert for anything out of the ordinary. I don't want Angie going to her old school anymore. I suggest you'll enroll her in the same school Michelle and Mandy are going to. And I want you to drive them to school for a while."

He questioned her with his eyes. "Are you okay with that?"

She nodded. "I was thinking the same thing, but I'm afraid. Do you really think they might go after Angie? She's just a child. She doesn't know anything."

"We haven't a clue why they murdered Michael. Until we do, no one is safe."

Her fingers dug into his arm. "Can we get police protection?"

"I doubt it. You've received no threats. This is just speculation."

"Does someone else have to be killed before anyone acts?"

"That's pretty well the way the system works. We don't have the manpower to watch over every citizen who might be in danger, imaginary or real."

"You're a cop, Jeff, for heaven's sake. There must be something you can do." She sounded exasperated and annoyed.

He knew how she felt and he regretted telling her about the sedan. There might not even be a connection between that car and Michael's murder. He mustn't get paranoid. He had to stay focused and impartial. Bending forward, he kissed Barbara on the forehead. "I'll talk to Maxine. She might be able to pull some strings. How are Mom and Dad dealing with it?"

"Dad went to lie down, and Mom, well, she's taking it better than I anticipated. She's always been strong. More so than Dad."

He went back with her into the living room and sat down beside Evelyn, Samantha's older sister.

Her husband, Fred, sat in the big chair, nursing a drink. He gave Jeff a nod. "It's a damn shame," he said with his deep voice. "If they catch those guys they should execute them immediately, not waste taxpayer's money with long trials and prison sentences. I saw this once on TV, in a news report. In China, they convicted this guy for tax evasion. After sentencing, they took him into the courtyard in the back and shot him. In the head. Now that's what I call justice. That's what we need in this country."

Jeff chuckled. "It sounds good in theory, but the chance of executing an innocent person is too great. Besides, don't you think executing someone for not paying his taxes is a little harsh?"

"That may be so, but it is not much different in our country. We don't execute tax evaders, but the courts punish white-collar crimes harsher than murder or robbery, especially when it comes to people who are trying to cheat on their taxes. You do something the government doesn't approve of, wow, you're a real criminal! But go and kill a couple of people, you can plead insanity and you go free."

"It's not as simple as that and you know it." Jeff shook his head, showing his disapproval. "At least everyone gets a fair trial. Like I said, we want to avoid killing or imprisoning innocent people."

"There is collateral damage in every war, and believe me, we're at war with the criminals in this country. And in other countries. It gets worse every year. We're losing control." He pulled a case from the inside pocket of his jacket and proceeded to shake out a cigarette, but Evelyn stopped him.

"Put that away, Fred. Barb doesn't like anyone smoking in her house."

Grumbling, he put his cigarettes away. "That's another thing. The non-smokers are taking over. All these minority interest groups are telling the majority of the population what they can or cannot do."

"Not smoking is better for your health," Evelyn said. "Smoking kills."

"Yeah, yeah. Everything pleasurable is bad for your health these days. All you hear is anti this, anti that. I'm going to vote for this new guy who's running for senate. What's his name? Ronald Larkin, that's him. He's thirty-five. A lawyer. Got some good ideas. His father was Senator Douglas Larkin. He just passd away. He was a good man. His son is trying to fill his vacated seat. They're Democrats, you know. I've never voted Democrats before, but this time I will."

Jeff suppressed a grin. Fred owned a cigar shop in Denver. Of course he'd be against nonsmoking or no drinking laws. If it were up to him, he'd make smoking dope legal.

"Uncle Jeff." Someone poked him. He looked up to see Mandy, Barbara's eleven year old daughter. "There is a lady at the door to see you."

"A lady?"

"Yes. She's blond and is very tall."

Montana.

"Thanks, Mandy." He turned to Evelyn. "Excuse me for a moment."

His ex-partner stood on the front veranda. She smiled when Jeff stepped out. "Hi, Jeff. Sorry to disturb you here, but I thought you'd want to be kept up to date."

"It's all right, Max. To be frank, I'm glad to get out of there. Michael's in-laws are not exactly a fun bunch. All they talk about is politics. And most of the stuff they're saying is nonsense. Bunch of rednecks. To them everything is black and white."

"I've known types like that." Her blue eyes studied him. "I apologize for not talking to you at the funeral, but you looked so…grieving, I didn't want to invade your private feelings."

He smiled. "I don't mind if you do. You can invade my private feelings anytime."

She cocked her head to one side, her eyes still on his face. "Wow. Are you missing me that much already?"

"Actually I do. We work well together, you and I. Couldn't ask for a better partner. I don't like my new job. They've put me behind a desk where I spent most of my time." He indicated the two chairs on the porch. "Come, let's sit down."

He watched her slide into the chair. When she crossed her legs, he caught a flash of white thigh and he realized how long he had been without a woman.

She looks quite attractive in her black dress.

"I've seen the medical examiner's report," she said. "They did find cocaine in Michael's and Samantha's system…"

"Impossible!" he interrupted.

"Let me finish. Apparently, it was injected into Michael after he'd been shot, but Samantha had it already in her before she was shot. According to the findings, neither one of them showed any damaged nose linings. They obviously never used drugs before."

"That means Michael was shot first and Samantha watched him die. Then they injected her and shot her. Those bastards!" Jeff clenched his fists, thinking of what Fred had said about executing murderers immediately. Suddenly, that idea didn't seem so bad. "Did the forensics team find anything else?"

"Nothing except what you already know."

"You don't believe my brother was a drug dealer, I hope?"

Montana shook her head. "No, I don't, but Sheppard thinks otherwise."

"I've never liked him. He's an idiot," Jeff said. "When can I get into my brother's house? Angie wants some of her things. And I want to look around myself. Maybe I'll find something."

"Captain Stoneman is sending in a cleanup crew tomorrow. They'll strip the beds and clean the furniture. There won't be much evidence left. Sorry." She lifted her shoulders, apologizing for something that wasn't her fault.

"That's okay. I'll be looking for personal things that only I can identify. I'll have a better chance of finding anything than the forensics team."

She got up from her chair. "I'll let you know. Take care, Jeff." She came up to him and kissed him on the cheek.

He watched her walk away, admired the movement of her round buttocks underneath her tight black skirt.

Funny, I've never looked at her this way. Never really thought of her as a woman. Why now all of a sudden?

Chapter Five

"Do me a favor and don't mention this to anyone, okay?"

"Sure." Strecker nodded and rolled down the squad car's window to light a smoke. He looked at Jeff. "Don't do anything you'll regret, Chartrand."

Jeff smiled grimly. "Don't worry. I won't unless I have to." He had spotted the black sedan in the parking lot of The Three Palms Casino. Before he walked up the steps to the building, he instinctively checked the gun under his armpit, made sure it moved easily out of its holster.

The guard by the door threw him a curious glance but didn't stop him. Jeff carried his badge inside his pocket. This was not an official visit. Walking into the casino, he noted the people at the slot machines and at the roulette tables. The place was packed. Gambling was good business, but Jeff knew this was not Galliano's main income.

He walked past the cages, glanced at the glistening bodies of the nude dancing girls and the half-drunken men watching them. They'd be screwing them on the tables if the law allowed it. When he arrived at the door with the Private sign on it, two burly guys barred his way.

"I guess you can't read signs. This is a private room, buddy," one growled. "Beat it!"

Jeff gave him a friendly smile. "I want to talk to your boss."

"He's busy. Besides, Mr. Galliano doesn't talk to anyone without an appointment."

"I'm making one. Right now."

"You'll have to talk to his secretary, but it's her day off."

"I don't really need the secretary to make the appointment," Jeff said, losing his patience.

"Then you won't get in, stupid. Now, get the fuck outa here! I'm not telling you again."

Jeff had been sizing up the guard, who outweighed his 235 pounds by at least 30. However, Jeff was solid muscle and in top shape, while the other one could have been a model for the Pillsbury Doughboy.

The second guard was a different story. He matched Jeff in height and physique. He had been silently watching, almost as if amused by the exchange between Jeff and his buddy.

Jeff decided to take him out first.

"You know something, I don't have the time to argue with you two clowns," he said and, with a sudden movement, he kicked sideways, smashing his heel into the guard's solar plexus to send him sprawling. Then he twisted around and drove his fist into the fat guy's belly.

Unprepared for the attack, his opponent let out a surprised grunt and folded forward. Jeff brought the edge of his right hand down, hitting the fat neck with great force. The big man slumped to the ground like a sack of flour. Jeff stepped over him and opened the door.

There were two people in the room. A man and a woman. The woman sat on the desk, the top of her dress down to expose her breasts. Behind the desk, sat a short, fat and completely bald man. His hands covered the woman's breasts.

The man looked up when Jeff walked in. "Who the hell are you?" he rasped. "And how did you get past my men?"

"They've decided to take a little nap." Jeff grinned. "They must have been tired of their job. Perhaps you're not paying them enough. My name is Jeff Chartrand. Does the name Chartrand ring a bell, Mr. Galliano?"

Galliano removed his hands from the woman's breasts. She slipped off the desk and pulled up her dress. "Leave us alone," Galliano told her. "Tell Alfonso and Tony to move their asses in here." Then he looked at Jeff out of black eyes hidden between folds of flesh. "What was your name again?"

"Don't pretend you didn't hear me the first time, Galliano," Jeff said calmly, keeping an eye on the fat man's right hand.

"It's Mr. Galliano to you. Now…what the fuck is so important that you have to bust into my office unannounced?"

"It's about my brother, Michael Chartrand. I believe you and he had business dealings."

"Michael Chartrand? Isn't that the guy who got wasted last week? He and his whole family?" His little pig's eyes glanced at the door. "Where the fuck are those two guys?"

"I told you they're asleep, but don't worry about your bodyguards. I didn't come here to kill you. If I wanted that you'd be dead already." Jeff kept his voice calm and steady. "Seems you do know who I'm talking about."

"I read the papers and I'm interested in everything that happens in this city. I remember this Michael Chartrand. Why shouldn't I? I remember every punk who owes me money. Your brother owes me five grand." He gave Jeff a calculating look. "You say you're his brother? Did you come to pay off his debt?"

"Why would my brother owe you money?"

"Playing blackjack, how else? Your brother lost it gambling. He promised to pay me two weeks ago. He failed to make his payment."

"And so you had him killed?" Jeff moved his hand toward his gun.

Galliano stared at him, and then he laughed. "Killed? You think I had your brother wasted? Listen, punk. I'm a legitimate businessman. I don't kill people over five lousy grand."

"Well, someone murdered my brother. I saw your sedan at the funeral."

"Yeah, so you did. What of it? I sent Tony to check up if your brother was really dead or if it was some scheme to get out of paying his debt. You wouldn't believe the kind of stuff people do just to stiff me." He eyed Jeff. "Actually, I'm glad you dropped by. He had property, your brother. Probably life insurance. His estate still owes me the money. With interest. I'd say I'm entitled to ten grand."

"Fuck you!" Jeff told him.

At that moment the door burst open and one of the bodyguards rushed in, gun in hand. He was alone. Doughboy was probably still out cold.

Jeff had his own gun already drawn and aimed at Galliano.

"Put your guns away. Both of you," Galliano bellowed, his rasping voice sounding like the grating of a rusty hinge. "What the fuck got into everyone? You!" He pointed at his bodyguard. "We talk later. I think I'm paying you too much to let some punk with a gun get past you to threaten my life."

"He surprised us, boss. The guy's a maniac. He kicked me like a fucking mule. I think he broke some of my ribs." He waved his gun around. "I didn't know he had a gun."

"Well, he does, and it's still pointing at my head. Put yours away, you moron. I don't want it to go off accidentally." Looking at Jeff, he said, "What the fuck are you? Some kind of crazy vigilante? I'll call the cops and have you arrested for threatening me at gunpoint, you crazy son of a bitch! Nobody threatens me and gets away with it."

Jeff holstered his gun after the bodyguard put his away. "I apologize for having troubled you, Mr. Galliano. I'm trying to find my brother's killer and I wanted to make sure I could eliminate you as a suspect."

"Are you a cop?"

Jeff shrugged. "Maybe I am."

"I have friends and connections," Galliano said. "You can't harass me like this. There are laws. Let me warn you. Don't show your face in here again, unless you have a warrant, you understand? I'll have my lawyer file a complaint."

"Why don't you do that, Mr. Galliano. In the meantime I'll be watching you."

"Get the fuck out of my office and off my property, you piece of shit. I still want my money, Chartrand. By the way, the amount just went up. Now you owe me fifteen G's. It'll be five more for every week the debt is unpaid."

"So what'll you do if you don't get paid? Have me murdered?"

"I told you, I don't shoot people, but with you I just might make an exception." He turned to his bodyguard. "Tony, accompany our guest out of the place and make sure he stays outside!"

"Don't bother, Tony," Jeff said amiably. "I'll find my way out of here. By the way, how are your ribs? A little tender, I hope. Next time I'll aim for your big nose."

"Fuck you!"

Strecker waited anxiously for him. "I was just going to come in after you, Chartrand. What the hell kinda business do you have with Galliano?"

"None whatsoever."

"I hope so. We've been watching him for a long time, but we don't have anything on him, nothing to implicate him, anyway. He's smart and he has friends in the mayor's office. There are rumors he has the DA in his pocket. Tread carefully and don't step on the wrong toes."

Jeff laughed without humor. "Right now I don't give a shit about whose toes I'll step on."

"That's what worries me." Strecker eased out of the parking lot. "I know what this is all about, Chartrand. You can't fool me. You're trying to find your brother's killer. I know how you feel, but they took you off the case for a reason. To prevent this kind of shit. In the end you'll only hurt yourself."

Jeff threw a glance at his new partner. "What would you do, Strecker?"

Strecker didn't answer for a while, and then he shrugged. "The same thing you're doing."

Chapter Six

"The courts have frozen all of Michael's assets and they confiscated the twenty thousand dollars that were found in your brother's closet."

"Why?"

Mallory sat hunched over behind his oversized mahogany desk, like a big, ugly bug, ready to launch itself out of its nest. He was Michael's attorney and the executer of the will. "To find out how your brother came into possession of twenty thousand dollars in cash. And then there is the question of the cocaine they found."

"My brother wasn't using, and neither was Samantha. The medical examiner already established that. It's a setup. Who's behind this court order?"

Mallory shrugged. "The DA. It's a criminal investigation. He doesn't need a reason. There is nothing I can do."

"How long are the assets going to be frozen?"

The attorney shrugged again, his eyes huge behind the thick lenses of his glasses. "Who knows? These things can take months. You know how slow the courts work. Michael's isn't the only case."

"I have to get into my brother's house. It's been three weeks. My niece is living with my sister and she needs her personal things, like clothing, her iPod, her computer games, and all the other stuff girls her age possess. Surely something can be arranged?" Jeff tried to keep his temper under control. He wanted to grab one of the ugly modern pictures hanging on the office walls and smash it over Mallory's shiny black bald head, squashing him like the bug he appeared to be. He knew this situation wasn't the man's fault, but Jeff had taken an instant dislike to him.

"I'll see what I can do," Mallory said. He looked at his watch. Rising out of his chair, he held out a hand. "I'm sorry to rush you off, but

I have another appointment already waiting in the front office. I have your number. I'll keep you informed if anything new develops."

Jeff took the hand, squeezed it a little harder than necessary and took some pleasure when he saw Mallory wince. "Try to hurry it." He smiled. "Otherwise I just might have to break into my brother's house."

Mallory didn't smile. "I wouldn't advise that, Mr. Chartrand. It will only complicate matters. Just be patient."

Jeff walked out of the plush office, wondering how much the attorney was going to end up with for his services. Anytime someone died, all the vultures moved in to get their share. Lawyers, funeral homes, real estate agents, debtors. And not to forget the IRS. The government was the hungriest and most savage of all the vultures.

He phoned Montana from his apartment. He hadn't heard from her for a week now. She seemed hesitant when he spoke to her. "Is everything all right?" he asked.

"I was told not to divulge any information to you."

"What the hell does that mean?"

"Apparently, they found stuff in Michael's possession that links him to terrorist groups."

"What?" Jeff was too stunned for a moment to even think about the implication of what she'd said. "Michael a terrorist? That's absurd!" He paused. "Max, I need to see that so-called evidence. This whole thing is becoming more bizarre from day to day."

"I don't think I can help you there, Jeff. Sheppard is not the only one on the case now. The Captain brought in a special team of investigators. They only share with us information they feel we should know about, which is very little."

"I spoke to Galliano," he told her.

"I know. That was a stupid thing to do."

"How do you know about it?"

"The DA phoned Captain Stoneman and reamed him out. The Captain isn't happy."

"Well, neither am I. Galliano told me Michael owed him gambling money, but he wouldn't go as far as killing someone for that. Not for a lousy five grand. I hope that puts Sheppard's theory about Michael being a drug dealer to rest."

"Not really. It only means Galliano probably wasn't involved in his murder."

"Shit! This whole thing doesn't make sense." Jeff cursed into the phone. "I still don't rule out Galliano. He's a criminal and I don't trust criminals."

"Forget about Galliano for now. We'll keep an eye on him, just in case. Sorry, I can't be of more help."

"You've done all you can, Max. Thanks." Jeff put down the phone and sat there, trying to digest what Montana had told him.

His brother communicating with a terrorist group? Impossible. He may not have known everything Michael did, but he would have at least suspected something like this.

Michael had been a true patriot. Fought in two wars. He believed in the war in Iraq, believed that America had done the right thing to invade Iraq and Afghanistan. He hated terrorists, hated the cowardly thing they had done September 11, 2001 to the American people. Fighting this global threat was his duty, to keep not only America free but also the rest of the world.

Sure, he had been discouraged after coming back home, but he would never have betrayed his country.

Never!

Jeff became angrier and angrier with the people who did this. His suspicion grew that there was much more hidden beneath what appeared to be a simple homicide. He needed to talk with someone to find out more about Michael's activities. Jeff knew most of Michael's friends. Maybe he should talk with the guys in Michael's shop.

He had not been able to bring himself to pick up his brother's tools and possessions he stored at his place of employment, but he would do it first thing in the morning.

* * * *

"I still can't believe it." Brent Cockburn wiped his large calloused hand across his thick, bushy mustache. "Every day when I come to work I expect Michael to walk through that door, wearing a big grin. He just finished fixing up that old corvette."

Jeff smiled. Brent was one of the mechanics Michael mentioned often. A big guy with a bigger heart. "Yeah, I still can't believe it myself." He looked at the huge red tools box. "You know, Brent, I have no use for all those tools. Besides, I couldn't get that monstrous thing out of here anyway. I live in an apartment. Not much room for something like that. Why don't you and the other guys split up the stuff."

"Are you sure? There's a lot of money invested here."

"I'm sure. At least that way the tools will be put to good use."

"Wow. Thanks." Brent held out his big hand. "Listen, if you ever need any work done on your vehicle, come see me, okay?"

"Okay, I will. I'll be taking the stuff out of Michael's locker. Maybe you can show it to me?"

"Sure. Just let me get the spare key from the office."

Jeff put Michael's coveralls and the other personal things he found in the locker into a large plastic bag. There was a small metal box with a lock on it, and he wondered what it contained. After talking to Brent and the other mechanics for a while, he drove to work. Having found out so little left him somewhat disappointed.

When he walked into the precinct, Lieutenant Beacher called him into his office. "I remember you from our rookie days, Chartrand. You were always a bit of a hothead. Captain Hutchington called you a cowboy without a hat, whatever that meant, but I don't believe it was a compliment. I got a call from Captain Stoneman. The DA is on his case. I don't think I need to tell you why. I'm talking about your little visit with Joseph Galliano. Next time you decide to go out on your own, clear it with me first."

"It was private, Lieutenant. Unofficial. I never flashed my badge once."

"That may be so, but you did this while on duty, and that makes it official." Beacher pulled a thick file out of his drawer. "See this, Chartrand? I'm keeping this in my desk so I can look at it once in a while. We've been trying to gather evidence on Galliano for a couple of years now. This file is full of crap. There's nothing in here I can use to even hold him for an hour. Your little excursion does not help our investigation."

"Well, I'm sorry, Lieutenant," Jeff apologized. "Next time I'll talk to you first."

"Good. Better yet, let's not have a next time. I'm putting you on fulltime desk duty for the duration of your stay with us. Stoneman thinks you're a good detective. Don't jeopardize your career."

That evening, when Jeff looked through Michael's possessions, he found a small photo album in a large envelope. It held pictures of a pretty dark-haired girl. Michael was in a couple of pictures, his arm around the girl's waist. It was the last picture that puzzled him. It showed Michael and the girl, but on this one, she held a baby in her arms.

He also found a small envelope with a key inside. It turned out to be the key to the metal box. When he opened the box, he discovered a journal. On the outside cover, it said Iraq. The pages were filled with Michael's neat handwriting. The box also contained a few pictures from Michael's war buddies and a list of names with addresses and phone numbers.

The most perplexing discovery was a key inside a small transparent plastic bag. Clearly a key to a deposit box.

When he checked the list of names, he counted ten names. One of the pictures was a group picture of ten soldiers wearing full battle gear. On the back of the picture, Michael had written The Ten Commandos, for Freedom and Justice.

From their talks, Jeff knew that these were the ten members of a Special Elite squad Michael had been a part of. All of these soldiers had received medals of Honor.

Reading through the list, Jeff came across the name Toby Miller. Corporal Toby Miller. He suddenly remembered hearing the name at Joseph's birthday party. The guy who had phoned Michael.

Jeff decided to talk to Miller. Unfortunately, he lived in Fresno, which was about a three-hour drive away.

His phone rang just as he decided to go to bed. Glancing at his watch, he noted that it was almost midnight.

It was Barbara on the other end of the line. "Jeff, I just got a call from some guy named Tony. He wanted to know when we would pay the twenty-five grand we owe his boss. I told him I didn't know what he was talking about. He said he'd phone back again to remind me. What the hell was that all about?"

Jeff suppressed a chuckle. Barbara didn't condone cursing, but when she did it herself, she was angry. This was a good sign. It meant she was slowly getting back to her normal self.

"Apparently, Michael lost five thousand dollars playing blackjack." When he heard Barbara's What? he said, "I was as surprised as you are.

Seems our brother had a bit of a gambling streak in him that we didn't know about."

"So what are we going to do?"

"Nothing. We have no legal obligation to pay any of Michael's debts. If there are any debts, legal ones, they'll be paid out of Michael's estate. There are no records of gambling debts, but I'm willing to pay it once everything is settled with the courts. Of course, we'll never pay out that kind of money. We'll pay the five thousand plus interest at a rate the courts will decide. Until then, don't worry about it."

"What if he calls again?"

"Tell him you'll send your big brother to break his nose."

"Really?"

"Really. Now, go to sleep."

Son of a bitch! Why did Michael have to go and lose money gambling? Galliano would not give up, but Jeff wouldn't let him harass or intimidate Barbara.

Chapter Seven

Lieutenant Beacher seemed almost relieved when Jeff told him he wanted some time off.

"Under the circumstances that is a wise decision. I'm surprised Captain Stoneman didn't order you to take a leave of absence. You're entitled, you know."

"At first, I thought staying and keeping on working might take my mind off, but I find it just makes matters worse. Maybe I'll go east for a while, do some fishing or whatever." Jeff had no interest in telling Beacher or anyone else about his true plans. This was something he needed to do without interference.

Back at home, he found a message on his answering machine from Michael's boss, asking Jeff to give him a call.

"This is Jeff Chartrand. You wanted me to phone you?"

"Yes. Sorry I missed you when you were here. Thanks for the tools. Very generous of you. Something your brother would have done. He was that kind of a man. The guys are happy and appreciative. Listen, I need to tell you something. Now that Michael and his wife are both dead, there is no more reason for secrecy. I had my accountant, upon Michael's request, deduct two hundred dollars every month from his paycheck and deposit it into an account with the National Bank of America. I don't know the reason for that, but he made me promise never to tell anyone, especially not his wife. We have all the deposit slips on file and if you like I can mail them to you."

Jeff had listened with a sense of despair. Why would Michael do something like that? Why would he need an account only he had access to? What did he do with that money?

"That would be great. Thanks."

"I'll need your mailing address."

Jeff gave it to him.

Michael, Michael. What have you done? What other secrets have you been hiding? Suddenly you're a stranger to me.

He looked up the phone number of Toby Miller, but when he dialed it, he received a message that the number was not in service.

The man could have moved. He phoned information, but there was no new listing for a Toby Miller. This left him with two choices. To take the long drive and check in with the local police department to find the man through his driver's license or he could phone Montana for help again.

He decided to phone Montana.

She called him back an hour later.

"Bad news, Jeff. According to the police report, a Toby Miller and his wife were found shot to death almost two weeks ago in their apartment. No arrests have been made. It seems the motive was robbery."

A cold shiver ran down Jeff's spine when Montana told him the news. Was this sheer coincidence that one of Michael's war buddies would get shot shortly after phoning Michael?

He didn't tell Montana about his suspicion that there may be a connection between the two murders, not until he found out more. Of course, Montana had a sharp mind. She could put two and two together. "You didn't tell me your interest in this Toby Miller, but I'm guessing it has something to do with Michael?"

"He's one of Michael's war buddies. I'm just following a hunch."

"A Detective Marvin Smith is handling the case. Maybe you'd want to drive there and have a talk with him. He sounded pretty amiable."

"I'll probably do that. Thanks, Max."

"No problem. Be careful, Jeff."

That settled it. He'd be going on this trip anyway. Since it was already late, he put it off until the next day.

* * * *

Detective Marvin Smith was indeed quite helpful, almost eager to share information. He looked young. As it turned out this was one of his first cases. Jeff told him about his brother's death and the similarities between the two murders. He also told him about his suspicion that it might have something to do with Iraq. "I may be on the wrong track, but right now I'm grasping at straws. I want to find my brother's killer."

"Don't blame you." The young detective scratched his chin. "We could work together, you and I. Share information. It might solve both murders. We have the dead man's answering machine. I was going through all the messages, hoping to find something…like death threats or stuff like that, but there was nothing there. Only messages from friends. I actually haven't followed up on them because I didn't think they were important. Except, one guy phoned three times. I remember the name. Dennis." He smiled. "I remember it because that's my brother's name."

Jeff pulled out his list of names. Sure enough, there was Dennis Kim. "Can I use your phone?" he asked.

"Go ahead. May I have a look at that list?"

Jeff gave it to Smith. Then he dialed Dennis Kim's number. The phone rang. A woman's voice answered after the second ring.

"Can I speak to Dennis, please?"

"I'm sorry," the woman said. "Dennis is in the hospital."

"Oh. Sorry to hear that. What happened? Did he have an accident?"

"No accident. Somebody tried to rob him. Beat him up with a baseball bat. May I ask who you are?"

A cold hand reached for Jeff's brain. It seemed like an odd coincidence to find another of Michael's war buddies had come to harm. "My name is Jeff Chartrand. My brother Michael served with your husband in Iraq."

"Dennis is not my husband. His wife divorced him two years ago. I'm just his friend. We're…living together."

"Is it possible to talk to Dennis? I really would like to. What hospital is he in?"

There was a short pause, and then the woman said, "I'm not sure if I should divulge that information to you. How do I know who you really are?"

"I understand. I really am Jeff Chartrand. My brother Michael is dead. Murdered. I'm a cop and I'm trying to find the people responsible."

"Maybe the same people tried to kill Dennis. The police said it was robbery, but I don't believe it." She paused again. "Maybe you are who you say, and maybe you just want to finish the job."

"I'm not blaming you for being suspicious. I'll let you talk to Detective Marvin Smith. I'm with him. Would you come to the police station to meet us?"

"I guess that would be all right."

"Okay. Here is Detective Smith." He handed the phone to the detective.

"She said she'll be here in an hour," Smith said, after hanging up. "Would you mind if I tag along?"

"I was hoping you'd say that, Detective."

"Call me Marvin." He smiled. "I'm still trying to get used to answering to Detective."

"You'll get used to it." Jeff smiled. "I'm Jeff." He liked this young man. With his attitude and open mind, he had a great future ahead of him.

They took Smith's patrol car. Jeff left his car in Smith's spot in the parking lot of the precinct.

The woman turned out to be petite and oriental looking. Quite beautiful, with a pretty smile. "I'm Connie Wu," she introduced herself and peered into Jeff's face. "You know there is a resemblance."

"A resemblance?" Jeff asked, perplexed.

"Dennis has an enlarged picture of the men he served with. He was a member of a special elite group. They called themselves the Ten Commandos, but you probably know that. Dennis was proud to be one of the ten men in that group. He talked a lot about his time in Iraq and his war buddies. I almost know them as intimately as he." She gave Jeff a smile. "You look very much like your brother. Dennis liked him a lot. He said Michael had always a smile on his face."

"He did," Jeff said. "He was the happier one of the two of us."

The trip to the hospital turned out to be disappointing.

"We've induced a coma," the doctor told them. "He's received extensive head injuries. He's lucky to be alive."

"Will he make it?" Smith asked.

"He should recover completely. The coma will speed up the healing process. How long until you can talk to him?" The doctor shrugged. "It's up to him, but he's a strong and healthy man, which will help tremendously."

Detective Smith gave Connie his card. "Phone me when he's ready."

She nodded. "I will." She looked at Jeff. "Nice meeting you. Too bad it had to be under these sad circumstances."

"Yeah, too bad." He watched her walking away and sighed. When she disappeared into the elevator, he said, "Lovely woman. Dennis Kim is very lucky."

Smith chuckled. "I have a feeling he would dispute that at the moment."

"Probably would," Jeff agreed.

"So what are you going to do next?" Smith asked.

"I'm not sure. There are seven more names on the list. I guess I'll try to get in touch with all of them."

"Do you by any chance have a picture of these people?"

"Yes, I do. Probably the same group picture Dennis Kim has. Why?"

"There was a name on the list you showed me. Ronald Larkin. It caught my attention."

When Jeff showed him the picture, Smith nodded. "Yeah, that's him. That is the son of the late Senator Douglas Larkin. This young man is vying for a place in the Senate, and he has a good chance of winning it."

"You know, now that you mention it, someone told me this before." Jeff looked thoughtful. "Maybe I should talk to him next."

"Well, let's get back to the precinct. I don't want anyone pulling your car away. Remember, you're parked in my designated spot." Smith smiled and began walking away.

After Jeff left the precinct, he looked for a place to eat. He found a small diner and had an early supper. Later, sitting in his motel room, he studied the list of names and tried to match them with the pictures. He knew Toby Miller and, of course, Michael. Both dead. Dennis Kim was obviously the oriental looking one in the picture.

Detective Smith had pointed out Ronald Larkin. Another man he knew, also dead, was Darrin Montana, Maxine's brother.

That left five names and five faces.

He remembered Michael's journal. Unfortunately, he had not brought it along, but it suddenly occurred to him how he could find out the names of the soldiers in the picture. He looked at his watch.

Eight P.M.

He dialed Connie's number. "Would you mind if I came to your house tonight? I know it's late, but this is important."

She gave him the address and directions how to find it. It was nine by the time he arrived there. Her apartment was on the fourth floor of a six-story building with a security system. Maybe that's why they had ambushed Dennis out in the open, instead of in his residence.

He had a feeling, Connie was lucky to be alive.

The apartment was small but nicely furnished. Jeff saw the large picture immediately. Some people hang oil paintings or prints on the wall; some like landscapes, some animals, some flowers; some prefer to decorate with photographs. It was clear that Dennis liked his memorabilia. There were pictures of helicopters, warplanes, tanks, ships, even a picture of a rocket launcher. Framed in the center of one wall hung a plaque and a medal.

Connie saw him looking and smiled. "He was proud of that one." She indicated the couch. "Sit down, Mr. Chartrand."

"Jeff. It's Jeff."

"Okay, Jeff. Would you like a drink?"

"A beer will do fine, if you have."

"I have. Dennis likes his beer also." She brought two bottles and two glasses. "He doesn't like cans. Beer should be in a bottle or served in a glass or mug, according to Dennis."

"Sounds like my brother-in-law. He's German. He doesn't like our American beer. Drinks only imports, German beer to be exact. In Germany they apparently don't allow any additives."

She poured her beer, and then she looked at him. "What can I do for you?"

"You told me you are familiar with all the men in the unit. I'm trying to put names to the faces in the picture, not too successfully, I have to admit. My brother never talked much about his time in Iraq."

She pointed to the large picture on the wall, and then she named the soldiers from left to right. "That tall, arrogant looking guy, that's Captain Ronald Larkin. He was the commanding officer of the unit."

"That's the guy who wants to be a senator."

"Right. The former Senator Douglas Larkin's son. Do you know him?"

"No, I don't. Detective Smith told me."

"Dennis didn't like him very much. He called him an arrogant, pompous son of a bitch. He's a lawyer. That big, heavyset guy, that's Staff Sergeant John Parker. Everyone called him Little John. Dennis referred to him as a huge bag of shit." She smiled. "Pardon me. He's Larkin's personal bodyguard. His father is General Mathew John Parker, retired."

"General Parker," Jeff mused. "Yeah, I know him. He was one of the generals pushing for the invasion of Iraq during the Gulf war. He wanted the US to smash Saddam Hussein while we had the country on its knees. Maybe we should have listened to him."

Connie didn't comment. She pointed to the man next to John Parker. "This is John MacKay. He was the medic. Then we have Private James Carrington, Brian McGee, Toby Miller, and Corporal Ethan Grey. He's a professional wrestler now. The guy beside him is Dennis, and the last two are your brother Michael and Corporal Darrin Montana."

"I know him also. We grew up together."

"Then you know he's dead. Killed in action. Apparently, by friendly fire. Dennis never talked much about him or how it happened."

"Neither did Michael. This is the first time I've heard he died by friendly fire." Jeff studied the picture for a while, repeating the names until he was sure he could remember them. He always had a good memory for names and faces. "Did Dennis ever talk about anything unusual that might have happened? Or of someone who might carry a grudge against any of the men in the unit?"

"Not really. He talked about skirmishes they ran into, the firefights, the ambushes, the many suicide bombers and all the dangers they faced on a daily basis. He even spoke of his missions, told me stuff that was probably never meant for a civilian to hear." She emptied her glass and looked at Jeff over the rim. "Want another beer?"

He shook his head. "No, thanks. Can't take that chance. I already had one for supper."

"Do you think the Iraqis sent a death squad to eliminate these men?" she asked. "Or maybe the CIA? Could it be they saw something they weren't supposed to know about?"

"I don't know what to think. Everything is possible."

She leaned forward. "This Ronald Larkin, he's running in the next election. Is there a chance someone wants him dead? In order to steer suspicion away from the real purpose they're killing off a few of the men who served with him? He might possibly be the next target. What do you think?"

Jeff smiled. "I'm not a conspiracy buff. I'm a police officer and I deal with facts." He rose. "Thank you for your information, Connie. If Dennis wakes up from his coma, let Detective Smith know. He'll get in touch with me."

She rose and stepped up to him, looked into face. "Do you really have to go already? Can't wait to get home to your wife?"

He smiled. "No wife is waiting for me. I'm not married. Not any more."

"Then what's the hurry? I feel lonely. Dennis and I, well, we're good friends and I'm fond of him, but we live together for convenience. He's...gay."

Jeff looked into her eyes. "What are you saying?"

She didn't answer, just took a step backward. Her hands pushed down the straps of her dress, let it slowly slide past her hips. Reaching behind her, she undid her bra and let it fall to the ground. Jeff stared at her breasts, large for an oriental woman, noticed the long, thick nipples. Pulling her dress further down, she exposed her white, lacey panties. She pushed them down with her dress, baring her pubic hair, which she had trimmed into a small heart.

"I want you to make love to me," she whispered, her almond eyes dark pools of promise. "Please, don't embarrass me by saying no."

He didn't know what to do, but the sight of her shapely nude body and her willingness didn't make it hard for him to decide. He smiled and nodded, stepping closer. She undressed him slowly, put every piece of his clothing on the table. When he was naked, she sank to her knees in front of him, fondling him gently.

He moaned when her lips touched his manhood and then opened to caress the length of his arousal. Releasing him, she rose, her breasts grazing his chest. He crushed her to him then, kissing her fiercely. Moaning, she led him toward the couch, pulled him on top of her, between her opening slender thighs. She cried out when he entered her and moved beneath him with unleashed desire, fuelling the hot flame inside him.

"Don't worry about getting me pregnant," she whispered. "I'm on the pill."

"Okay."

Neither of them spoke after that. There was no need. The only sounds in the room were their moans and cries of passion and the creaking of the springs, as their bodies thrashed wildly in the age-old language of aroused desire.

When he drove back to the motel, his mind in turmoil as he thought about what just happened with a woman he barely knew and the accusation that Michael might have ties to a terrorist group.

Maybe what Connie said about conspiracies wasn't that farfetched after all.

Chapter Eight

He drove back the next morning. As soon as he arrived home, he phoned Montana.

"What did you find out?" she asked.

He told her. He also told her about Connie's theories. Montana stayed silent for a while. "One might draw those conclusions," she said after a long pause, "but it's only speculation. You have no proof of anything."

"Not yet, but I will find some," Jeff said.

"Tread carefully, Jeff. You could be entering dangerous territory. The Feds have been sniffing around, asking questions about you."

"About me? What the hell! Why didn't you tell me?"

"I'm telling you now."

"Why would they drag me into this?"

"I don't know."

"It proves someone doesn't want me digging."

That evening Jeff sat down to read Michael's journal. The first pages were filled with Michael's thoughts as he described some of the terrible things he witnessed and was part of. He talked about every man in his unit and how well they all worked together.

Each one of us is responsible for the smooth operation of our unit.

Then something must have happened, an incident he never mentioned but hinted at. One reference to Darrin Montana read Darrin doesn't want to stay silent any longer. I told him to keep his mouth shut for the good of the unit and for his own safety. It happened; there is nothing we can do about it now. Casualties of War. I will be responsible for my own mistakes.

That's where the journal ended. The rest of the pages were missing.

Jeff studied the pictures of the dark-haired girl and the baby, wondering who they were and why Michael would have them in his possession. He didn't find any reference in the journal. She was clearly an Iraqi girl, as was evident by the clothing she wore.

A fling? Hardly. American soldiers didn't fool around with the local girls. This was not Vietnam. The Muslims had a totally different morality. Many girls had been stoned to death or hanged by their own families for bringing shame when they had sexual relations with the American Dogs, the Infidels.

He went to bed, tired and agitated.

Instead of finding answers, he had been presented with more questions.

* * * *

Since it was Sunday, he decided to sleep in. He was still tired from the trip, but he wasn't allowed to sleep for long. His phone rang at nine o'clock.

It was Barbara. "I was hoping you'd be back," she said. "That guy phoned again. Said we owed a Mr. Galliano thirty thousand dollars. I told him to stop bothering us otherwise I'll send my big brother, like you told me. He got real nasty, asked if the three girls were still virgins. It would please him immensely to change that. And he'd fuck me as a bonus."

Jeff cringed when she said that. He wasn't used to hearing her talk that way. She never talked like that.

"So you'd better pay that man a visit. He scares the hell out of me."

"I'll look after it. Don't worry, Barb."

"Don't worry? Jeff, this man wants to hurt our daughters. Maybe he's the one who murdered Michael." She sounded upset, almost hysterical.

"He didn't, I'm pretty sure of that. He's just a low-life punk. Like I said, I'll take care of him."

"When?"

"Today," he said grimly.

Galliano, that slimy bastard! Jeff didn't care what kind of connections he had to any so-called influential people. He was a criminal and Jeff wouldn't stand by doing nothing while his hired muscle threatened and intimidated his family.

He picked up the phone, dialed the number of his precinct. Then he told the desk sergeant on duty to give Lieutenant Beacher a call and tell him that Jeff Chartrand is going to pay Joseph Galliano a visit. He hung up before the sergeant could comment on it. Then he showered, dressed, made sure his gun was loaded and in its holster, and then he headed for the 'Three Palms Casino'.

Doughboy Alfonso seemed to have the day off. Only Tony stood by the door. His hand went into his jacket when he saw Jeff marching up to him, but before he could draw his gun, Jeff punched him in the face. He heard cartilage breaking as the big man's nose flattened under the impact.

"I told you I'd break your nose," Jeff said grimly. He hit the other man in the stomach, twice, and then he kicked him in the groin. When Tony sank to his knees, Jeff grabbed him by the hair and brought his face close enough to smell the alcohol on the big man's breath. "If you ever phone my sister again and threaten her and the girls, I'll kill you, you son of a bitch. You tell your boss he'll get his five grand with reasonable interest when the courts decide to release my brother's property. Is that clear?"

Jeff let go of the other one's head and backhanded him.

Tony moaned loudly and tried to get up. Jeff pushed him down again. "Stay down, you piece of shit, and answer me!"

"It wasn't my idea. Mr. Galliano ordered me to do it. He's the boss." He wiped his hand across his bloody face. "You broke my nose, you mother-fucker!"

"Watch your mouth, or I'll break all your beautiful front teeth." Jeff pulled back his fist, but he finally brought his anger under control and stepped back. "You tell Mr. Galliano what I told you. Next time I'll come for him. And remember, I don't make idle threats."

He made it back to his car before the cruiser pulled into the parking lot. He walked over to the two patrol officers and flashed his badge. "There was a bar-fight in there, nothing serious. I took care of it. No need for you fellows to get involved."

"Are you sure?" Both officers were young, one of them a rookie, he guessed. It was Sunday. The older veterans had the day off.

"I'm sure. I'll take care of the paperwork."

"Sounds good to me. I hate these bar-fights. You never know what you may walk into."

He drove home, feeling good but also a bit wary. Galliano would not take this lightly. There'd be consequences, but Jeff was willing to face them.

* * * *

The material Michael's boss promised to send came Monday in the morning's mail. Jeff discovered a thick wad of deposit slips from a local branch of the National Bank of America in the envelope. They dated all the way back to Michael's return from Iraq. However, Jeff couldn't do much with this information; he had a bank account number but no way to access the account. He phoned Michael's lawyer, Mallory, and asked him to find out what happened to the money Michael deposited to this account.

Mallory called him back a couple of hours later, telling him that there was no way of knowing because the amount of two hundred dollars was withdrawn as soon as it was deposited. At a bank machine.

Another dead-end road.

Jeff cursed silently. Whichever way he turned, he ran into an obstacle. He got out Michael's list of names and then he studied the pictures.

Ronald Larkin. Captain Ronald Larkin. Now an aspiring politician. He would have many enemies, who may want to see him dead.

According to Michael's notes, Larkin lived in LA, but that address could be old. However, it shouldn't be hard to find a man who was running for office.

* * * *

When his phone rang, it wasn't Captain Stoneman, as expected, but Montana. "Jeff, what the hell were you thinking? You can't just go around beating up people. Stoneman is furious. He's ready to have you arrested for battery and aggravated assault."

Jeff chuckled into the phone. "So why doesn't he?"

"I asked him not to, but it didn't take much convincing. He knows you're not yourself these days and you're acting under duress. You're a good cop. He wants you back when this is over." She paused, and then she said with a low voice, "Don't do this kinda shit. You're in enough trouble already. I'm worried about you, Jeff."

He smiled, even though she couldn't see his face. "Well, it's nice to know you care, Max," he said softly.

"Of course I do, you big dumb lug."

"Since I have you on the phone I'll ask you for a favor. I'd like to get in touch with a Ronald Larkin. He's the guy who wants to be a senator. He also happens to be one of Michael's war buddies. In fact, he was the CO of Michael's unit. Can you find out how I can reach him?"

"Are you suspecting he is involved?"

"No, not directly, but he may be on the killer's list."

"Okay, I'll see what I can do."

"And Max…don't tell Stoneman. I don't want him to drop of a heart attack."

"All right," she said, laughing.

It didn't take long before she phoned him back. "You're in luck. Larkin is actually in town. He's giving a speech in the Radisson Hotel tomorrow night."

"That's better than I ever expected. Hey, Max, do you want to go and listen to some political speeches?" he asked on an impulse.

She hesitated for a moment. "Sure, why not. Maybe I can keep you out of trouble."

He spent the evening studying the pictures and reading Michael's journal again, in case he missed something the first time. Before he went to bed, he watched the news. There was nothing new, except for the usual reports of accidents, forest fires, shootings and stabbings. The only thing that aroused his interest was a short interview with Senator Osborne, who was a great supporter of the war in Iraq. He talked mostly about the inevitable invasion of Iran, which seemed to be his favorite topic.

Jeff remembered his conversation with Samantha's brother, Frank, at the funeral. He had mentioned Senator Osborne. Jeff didn't agree with the Senator. The occupation of Iraq was more than enough trouble for the US to handle. Invading Iran would be a grave mistake with almost certain dreadful consequences. Iran had pacts with Russia and China, who had more than just a passing interest in Iran's oil. They couldn't let the Americans gain control over the oil supplies in the Middle East.

* * * *

When he came home from breakfast the next morning, he found a message on his answering machine from a man with an eastern accent.

"Hello, Mr. Chartrand, my name is Basheer Khalil. I am the secretary for the local Muslim community. Could I please incite you to give us a call?" He gave his phone number for Jeff to make an appointment.

Well, this is beginning to get interesting. What possible connection could Michael have with the Muslim community?

Since he had nothing planned for the day, he decided to give the man a call. "Jeff Chartrand here," he announced himself.

"Ah, yes, Mr. Chartrand. I'm glad you called back. There is a matter of some urgency I would like to discuss with you."

"Does it have something to do with my brother Michael?"

"Yes, most definitely, but I don't want to discuss this on the phone."

"Will one o'clock this afternoon be fine?"

"Excellent. See you then."

Jeff was looking forward to the visit with some apprehension. Today he might just find out something about his brother he may not want to know.

Basheer Khalil was a small, dark-skinned man with a hooked nose. Although he spoke with a heavy accent, his words were precise and somewhat stilted.

He took Jeff into a small office in the back of the mosque. "Excuse the mess," he said, apologizing for the boxes of files standing everywhere. "We are just going through a re-organization." He hesitated and chuckled. "Actually, that is not quite the truth. We have had a visit from the FBI. Being a Muslim carries its hazards these days in America." He held up a hand. "I mean no disrespect. It is still a great country."

"It is," Jeff agreed. "Unfortunately, people are a bit jittery. And not without a reason, you have to admit."

"Have a seat, Mr. Chartrand." Khalil pulled out a chair and indicated for Jeff to sit down. He seated himself behind a small desk. "I guess you're wondering what you're doing here?"

"You're correct. I am."

"Your brother Michael, he was a man of honor. A good man. We are sorry to know he has been murdered."

"What is your interest in my brother?" Jeff asked, shifting uneasily in his chair.

"I don't want to, how do you say…beat around the bush. Your brother made a donation of two hundred dollars every month to our mosque. We kept ten dollars for administration fees and one hundred-ninety dollars we sent to the International Organization of Aids for Iraq."

Jeff didn't show the shock he felt hearing this revelation. Keeping his face neutral, he asked, "Why would my brother donate two hundred dollars to your community every month?"

"Not to us. You see, the IOAI sends all the money to Iraq where it is given to certain families. We don't know who received your brother's money, only the IOAI has that on file." His dark eyes studied Jeff. "From your reaction I see that you were unaware of this."

"Obviously it was his secret. Nobody knew. I just would like to know what reason he had for doing this."

"I'm sure he had a good reason. The IOAI is a charity founded strictly to help Iraqi citizens who have been touched by the war. They have many American contributors." He smiled. "And not all are Muslims."

"Why are you telling me this, Mr. Khalil?"

"We want to know if we can count on this donation to continue. Did your brother provide for it in his will?"

Jeff shook his head. "I'm not aware of anything, and I cannot give you an answer immediately unless I know for certain what this money was used for. My brother must have had a valid reason for it. He never shared this with anyone in the family. How do I know the IOAI is not a front for an organization with connections to the Al Qaeda?"

"I assure you that is not the case, Mr. Chartrand."

"I only have your word. All this is a little too much for me to digest." He rose from his chair. "Nice talking to you, Mr. Khalil. I'll be in touch."

"Maybe I can find out for you who the recipient of this money is?"

"It would help, but until I know more there is nothing I'm going to promise." He turned and walked out of the building.

What in heaven's name had Michael been involved in?

He stopped for a bite to eat, and then he drove home. He picked up Montana shortly after six.

Chapter Nine

She looked stunning in her long red dress. It clung to her trim figure like a second skin, accentuating her narrow waist and plump buttocks. Looking at her, he wondered if she wore any panties underneath the thin material.

"Red suits you," he said, opening the car door for her.

She laughed throatily. "It's my long blond hair. I've decided to wear it loose tonight."

"You look ravishing." He grinned. "I've always loved long hair on my women."

"Does that mean I'm your woman?" she asked, smiling impishly.

"That's right. For tonight, anyway."

She looked him over. "You don't look so bad yourself in that dark suit. I didn't know you wore one except at funerals." Her face became serious. "Sorry, I shouldn't have said that. It didn't come out the way I meant it."

"It's all right, Max." He walked around the car and slipped into the driver's seat. "How's Detective Sheppard these days?" he asked after he was seated.

"Frustrated. He's run into a roadblock. Actually, he's still clinging to his theory that the murders were a drug deal gone sour."

"He's an asshole. Who would leave all that dope and twenty thousand in cash behind? Come on! This was an assassination. I firmly believe that now. I just don't have enough details to put it all together."

She glanced at him. "Are you telling me you have a suspect?"

"Unfortunately, no."

"In other words you know nothing."

"Not quite true. I found out that Michael was donating two hundred dollars every month to a Muslim organization." He didn't look at her, but he could feel her eyes on him, knew she was trying to make sense out of what he just told her.

"Are we talking about a terrorist group here?" she finally asked.

"The group calls itself International Organization of Aids for Iraq. Maybe you can check them out for me."

"I certainly will." She let out a deep sigh. "It's funny, actually. You think you know someone and then suddenly you find out you don't really. He was your brother, for Christ sake. How could you not have had at least an inkling?"

Jeff shrugged. "Michael was good at keeping secrets. He should have worked for Intelligence."

"You don't believe Michael was involved with terrorists?" she asked.

"Not Michael. There has to be another explanation."

"I'm beginning to believe in your conspiracy theories."

Luckily, the rally was open to the public and not just by invitation only. Jeff and Montana sat through two hours of listening to political speeches. Ronald Larkin was a charismatic speaker. Tall and handsome, and a smile that would have looked good on the cover of a fashion magazine, he held his audience captive, and Jeff was ready to vote for the man.

In spite of that, Jeff realized that Larkin was a phony, like the majority of politicians. All the promises he made, he couldn't keep most of them, but it all sounded good and convincing.

After the question period, Jeff asked Montana to stay at the table, while he tried to get some time alone with Larkin.

"Watch out for that big guy with him," Montana said. "He looks mean."

Jeff grinned at her and headed for the rear of the room to intercept Larkin.

The bodyguard spotted Jeff first and barred his way. He squinted at Jeff and said, "You look familiar. Do I know you?"

Jeff gave him a friendly smile. "Not me but my brother Michael. People say we look alike. You must be Little John."

"Only to my friends," the man growled. "What is it you want?"

"I'd like to speak with Mr. Larkin. It's about my brother."

"Yeah, well, make an appointment."

"This is important. There may be an attempt at Mr. Larkin's life. Maybe yours, also."

"What's going on, John?" Jeff stepped to the side and stood looking at Ronald Larkin. "I'm Jeff Chartrand. Michael Chartrand's brother."

"Michael Chartrand?" Larkin's eyes seemed to glaze over for a moment. "Oh, yeah, right. He was in my unit. Good man. How is Michael these days?"

"He's dead."

"Dead? I'm sorry to hear that. I liked him. He was a dedicated soldier. How did it happen?"

"Someone shot him. I'm trying to find out who." Jeff looked around the room. "Can we go somewhere more private?"

"Of course we can. There is a small bar at the end of the lobby. It's quiet there. We should be undisturbed. John, lead the way."

Jeff followed them out of the room. Before he walked out, he looked for Montana, saw her watching him. He lifted his hand. She nodded and got up.

As they walked down the corridor, Montana came toward them. She stopped and smiled. "All right if I join you?"

John opened his mouth, but before he could say anything, Jeff said, "She's with me."

Montana hooked her arm into Jeff's. "He's so helpless without me." She laughed and looked at Larkin. "Sometimes I wonder how he makes it through the day when I'm not with him. Do you have a woman who looks after you, Senator Larkin?"

Larkin laughed and looked at Jeff. "I like her. Anyone who calls me Senator is my friend."

They found a table in a corner and sat down. "Are you a Democrat, Jeff?" Larkin asked.

"Not really. I'm not into politics and, frankly, I don't care who's in power, as long as the laws are just and the people we vote for honest, putting the welfare of the country before their own interests. In the words of President John F. Kennedy Ask not what your country can do for you, ask what you can do for your country."

Larkin clapped. "Bravo. Spoken like a true Democrat. I hope I have your vote."

"Any friend of Michael's can count on me." Jeff smiled. "You can't be all bad."

"Well, thank you, Jeff." He bent forward. "Now tell me your real reason for being here." His eyes were suddenly wary, watchful. "Is this an official visit?"

"Official? No. Why do you ask?"

"I know you're a cop. Michael told me all about you. I make it a point to know everything about my men, even their families."

"I'm actually a homicide detective, but I'm not here on official business. I'm just trying to find out why my brother was murdered. I came to warn you."

"Warn me?" Larkin's face showed surprise.

"Yes. Toby Miller has also been murdered, and there has been an attempt on Dennis Kim's life. Looks to me someone is trying to kill off the men in your unit. You may be next."

"I'm not worried. I have a good bodyguard in Little John here. He keeps me safe." He winked. "And I'm not exactly helpless, you know. After all, I was a soldier."

"Don't take this too lightly, Captain Larkin. I read part of Michael's journal and I get the impression that something happened while you were in Iraq, something that may have spawned these murders."

"You have Michael's journal?" Larkin eyed him speculatively.

"Just part of it and a key to a deposit box."

"Really? Anything else?" Larkin seemed suddenly very interested.

"Pictures and a list of names."

"What kind of pictures?"

"Of a girl. An Iraqi girl. And a baby. Do you know why Michael would have a picture of an Iraqi girl? Who is she?"

Larkin shrugged. "I can't tell you unless you show me the picture. Maybe you can bring the stuff you have to me. John or I can look through it and, maybe, it'll jog our memories. Come to think of it, maybe you should hand over all this stuff to the Military anyway. If you give it to me, I will make sure it gets to the right department. There might be information that shouldn't fall into the wrong hands. Details of our missions for instance."

"So far I haven't read anything of great importance. Like I said, I only have part of the journal. If I can locate the rest of it I might just take you up on your suggestion." Jeff rose. "Thanks for your time…Senator." He winked. "I guess we'd better get going. I know you're a busy man."

"No problem. I always have time for the friends and families of my men. We are all brothers, you know. We looked out for each other. We still do."

As they walked away, Montana said under her breath, "What a pompous, arrogant ass. Did you see him undressing me with his eyes?"

Jeff chuckled. "You do look delectable in your tight red dress, Max. How can you blame the man? He's got good taste. What do you say, we go and have a drink, since we're here already and all dressed up?"

"Sounds good to me."

After her fifth gin and tonic, Montana seemed to be in good spirits. She kept touching his hand and she laughed a lot. Jeff took his time with his beer. He had never been a big drinker, not since his army days. Besides, he was the driver.

He liked her laugh. This was a new side of her and he found himself attracted to her.

"Let's go home," she said.

He nodded, amused by her tipsy condition.

Before she got into the car, she stepped close to him, put her arms around his neck and kissed him, forcing her tongue into his mouth. Then she pressed herself tightly against him. He had to admit she felt good in his embrace.

"What was that all about?" he asked when they broke apart.

Her blue eyes stared into his. She said nothing, only smiled.

In the car, she said suddenly, "I want to spend the night with you, Jeff."

Her words took him by surprise. He glanced at her. "You're drunk, Max. You don't know what you're saying."

"I'm not drunk, only a little maybe. And I know exactly what I'm saying. Never been surer." Her hand reached out to touch his neck. "Don't you find me desirable?"

"Desirable?" He chuckled. "Hell, Max, you drive me crazy. I've had a boner all night and right now, I'd like to do nothing else but rip off that red dress of yours and ravish you. Right here in the car."

"Well, then what's the problem? We're both adults, neither one of us is married. When was the last time you got laid?"

Last Friday. He couldn't tell her for obvious reasons. It had been a long time before that. "I can't remember." He grinned in the darkness of the car. "And you?"

She slapped him on the arm. "A gentleman never asks a lady that question, but if you must know, I can't remember either."

When they entered his apartment, Jeff saw the blinking light of his answering machine but ignored it. He went to the liqueur cabinet and poured himself a brandy. He turned to see Montana standing in front of him, her red dress pooling around her ankles. His suspicion was confirmed. She hadn't worn any panties. No bra, either.

"Wow," was all he could say.

She smiled wickedly and stepped out of her dress. He stared at her full breasts and smooth flat belly, and let his gaze linger on the shaved, plump pubis between her slim thighs.

"Get undressed," she said softly.

She watched him as he shed his clothes and ran her tongue across her red lips when he dropped his briefs. Then she stepped up to him and pressed her nude warm body against his, capturing his erection between her soft thighs. Her tongue snaked into his mouth when she kissed him.

After breaking the kiss, she took the brandy glass from him and lay down on the floor. Pouring the brandy between her breasts, she looked at him from lowered lids.

"Don't just stand there and gawk at me," she said throatily. "You know what I want. Come, lick it up." Some of the brandy dribbled across her belly, down to her pubic area.

He dropped between her spread legs and bent over her to dip his tongue into the deep cleft between her breasts. She moaned and dug her fingers into his hair.

"Gently," she whispered. "Take your time."

Licking her breasts, he tasted the brandy on her soft skin. Slowly moving across her belly, he dipped his tongue between her labia. She moaned deeply and squirmed, pressing her pussy against his face. "Yes," she sighed, "that's it. Don't stop, just don't stop."

His penis was a hard mast and it took all of his control not to drive it into her flowing pussy, but he kept licking her until she had a couple of orgasms before he moved up and lay between her clutching thighs. When he slid into her, she let out a satisfied cry and wrapped her legs around his thighs, pressing her heels into his buttocks.

They didn't speak for a long time. Soft whispering sounds escaped her lips as she moved underneath him.

"Don't hurry, lover," she moaned. "Please, don't hurry."

She cried out softly when he finally shuddered between her clutching thighs and held him tight. They fell asleep in each other's arms, exhausted and satisfied.

Chapter Ten

Montana left his apartment early in the morning. She wanted to go home first and change. "Can't go to work in this dress," she joked. "I'd be arrested for soliciting."

She blew him a kiss when she walked out of the door. Before she closed it, she turned around and said, "I wore it especially for you, just so you know." Then she was gone.

Jeff chuckled to himself. This was a side of her he had never seen before. Soft, cuddly, seductive, and utterly feminine. Until now, she had always seemed cool and collected. A good-looking woman but not a woman with a lot of passion.

She was a damn good cop and he'd never really thought of her as a sexy, desirable bed partner.

A huge grin suddenly spread across his face and he stretched out on the bed, which they had finally tumbled into after waking up on the hard floor.

She was a sex kitten. Who would have thought? Maxine Montana, the love-goddess. Damn!

When he ate breakfast, he remembered to check his answering machine.

It was Detective Marvin Smith. "Hi, Jeff. I hoped to catch you at home. Dennis Kim has regained consciousness. His girlfriend called this afternoon. Thought I'd let you know. Maybe you want to come and talk to him. Call me back."

Deciding to drive there right away, he phoned Montana to let her know, but he got only her answering service. "I'm driving up to Fresno. I should be back tomorrow noon." After leaving the message, he phoned Detective Smith.

The trip didn't seem to take as long as the last time. He felt elated and happy, and he listened to classical music all the way.

What a good roll in the hay does to a man, he thought, amused. Especially with a woman like Montana. With an almost guilty conscience, he thought of Connie. Sex with her had been great also. Perhaps they could get together again. After all, he and Montana hadn't made any commitments to each other. It had been a one-time thing and might never happen again.

Smith was in his office. Together they drove in Smith's cruiser car to the hospital where Connie met them. Her almond eyes lit up a little when she saw Jeff, but her face stayed serious.

"He hasn't said much," she told them. "The doctor said he's suffering from memory loss. His memory may come back, but he's not sure."

Dennis Kim looked up when they walked in. He smiled at Connie, but when he saw Jeff, he seemed suddenly exited. "Michael?" he said.

Jeff stepped closer. "I'm Jeff. Michael's brother."

It was apparent the other man didn't hear what he said. "How are you, buddy? It's been a while." He tried to sit up but fell back. Smiling weakly, he said, "I guess they got me. Listen, I gave it to Linda. It's safe with her."

"What did you give to Linda?"

"I never told John. I only told him about your journal and the pictures."

"John Parker?"

"No. Not Parker. MacKay." Kim chuckled. "It doesn't matter because John is dead. He wasn't really here. Only in my imagination."

"He thinks you're Michael," Connie whispered beside Jeff.

"Well, I'm glad it's safe," Jeff said. "Listen, Dennis, who did this to you?"

"Did what to me?"

"Who beat you up?"

"Nobody beat me up. I can defend myself." He moaned quietly. "This war is going to kill us yet. Am I hurt badly?"

Connie touched his cheek. "You were but you're recovering now."

"Good. I remember something important," Kim said. "You and I aren't the only ones who know. McGee knows. I didn't tell John about

McGee." He closed his eyes. "I'm very tired. I think I'll catch some shuteye. Gotta be ready in the morning. Important mission ahead."

"I think you should leave," the nurse said behind them. "He's been sedated and is living in his own little world. You'll have to give him more time. I told his other visitors the same thing."

"What other visitors?" Jeff asked.

"Those two FBI agents."

"When were they here?"

"Last night."

"I see." Jeff looked at Kim who seemed to have gone to sleep. "I guess we can't do much here."

"I'm sorry," Connie said. "You've come all this way for nothing."

"Maybe not. Dennis said that he gave it to Linda. Do you know what he meant by that?"

She shrugged. "Linda is his ex-wife. I suppose he's talking about her. We never really discussed his marriage. I haven't the faintest idea what he means."

"Where does his ex-wife live?" Jeff asked.

Connie shrugged again. "I don't know. Somewhere in Fresno, that's all I know. She married the guy she fooled around with while Dennis was in Iraq, putting his life on the line, defending her freedom. She's a bitch and didn't deserve a guy like Dennis anyway."

Maybe she left him because he's gay, Jeff thought but didn't say it. "I guess you wouldn't know her last name?"

"No, I don't."

"If she has a driver's license I can probably trace her," Detective Smith suggested.

"All right, let's do it."

When Jeff said goodbye to Connie, she looked at him and said with a low voice, "Drop by my place before you drive home, okay?"

He and Smith drove back to the police station. It didn't take the young detective long to find out that Linda now went by Reese, her maiden name. She was married to a Larry Yaremko.

"I guess she's one of those modern women whose husband's name isn't good enough. One wonders why they bother to get married instead of just living together," Smith commented.

"Maybe she's afraid this new marriage won't work out. If it doesn't then she saves herself the trouble of changing all her identification papers again," Jeff said.

"I don't buy that argument. I'd be a little apprehensive if my wife didn't want my name." He shrugged. "Maybe I'm just old fashioned. My mother took my father's name. I expect my wife to do the same. Keep the tradition and keep it simple. I pity the children of such families. Forever explaining why their mother has a different name."

"Did you know that in the Arab countries women don't take their husband's name?" Jeff asked.

"I didn't know that, but then I don't really know anything about those people. Even if that is so, this is America, with old traditions. Let's not change them and adopt customs from other countries."

Jeff smiled at Smith's little tirade. "For a young man you're quite rigid, my friend," he said, "but perhaps it's a good thing. Some people have to make sure our country keeps the old values our forefathers fought so hard to achieve. Well, anyway, at least now we know where Linda lives. I'd like to give her a call."

Jeff introduced himself on the phone and gave her the news about her ex-husband Dennis. "He told us he gave you something, but he never said what it was. I wonder if I could come by."

"No need to. I can give it to you over the phone. It's just a number. I'm keeping it in my jewelry box because he told me to guard it with my life. If you can wait a moment I'll get it for you." She hesitated. "Why would anyone do such a thing to Dennis? Was he the victim of a gay-bashing?"

"We don't know. The police are still trying to find out."

"I hope they find the ones who did that." She gave him the information he wanted.

It was an address and a number. Detective Smith studied it for a moment when Jeff showed it to him. "Looks like a safety deposit box number and the address of a bank. In which city, though?"

"I know that address," Jeff said. "It's the bank my brother dealt with and it's in Sacramento." He pulled a key from his pocket. "I'll bet this is the key to that box. Wonder what I'll find in there?"

He thanked Detective Smith for all his help and promised to keep in touch, and then he drove to Connie's apartment.

She opened the door and smiled at him. "I was hoping you'd come by." Taking him by the hand, she pulled him toward the bedroom. "I thought we'd make love in more comfortable surroundings this time." She opened the thin kimono she wore and let it slide to the floor. She was naked underneath.

On the night table beside the bed stood two glasses filled with red wine. Naked, she walked to the table. The sight of her round buttocks aroused him tremendously. She picked up the glasses, handed one to Jeff.

"Have a glass of wine with me," she whispered. "Alcohol always lets me shed my inhibitions." She looked at him over the rim of the glass as she drank. "Drink it all," she said. "It will help you relax."

Thoughts of Maxine popped into his head and he felt guilty, almost as if he were about to cheat on a lover, but when Connie kissed him hungrily, she made him forget all about Maxine.

Like the last time, she undressed him and then she made him sit at the edge of the bed. Facing him, she straddled him and sheathed herself on his erection. She was as wild as the first time, wild and full of fire.

They spent the rest of the afternoon in her bed, and for a little while, he didn't have to think about anything but this passionate woman who gave him pleasure beyond anything he had experienced in a long time. For a little while, he was happy.

Later, they had supper together and, even though Connie almost begged him to spend the night, he decided to drive home. "It's better this way," he said. Then he kissed her gently.

* * * *

It was late when he finally pulled into his parking space. Looking at his watch, he noted that it was 11:35 P.M., too late to phone Montana.

He knew something was wrong when he opened the door to his apartment and found the lock busted. The pillows on the couch were shredded, pieces of the fluffy white insides spilled onto the green leather. His liquor cabinet stood open, bottles lay smashed on the floor, the liquid staining the carpet red and yellow. The smell from the spilled liquor still lingered in the air.

Drawing his gun, he walked stealthily down the short corridor to his bedroom, but whoever had broken into his apartment was long gone. The bedroom lay in shambles. All the drawers had been pulled out of the dresser and night table, their contents emptied onto the floor.

Suits and shirts from the closet were heaped in an untidy mess on the bed.

Maybe I should have spent the night with Connie. At least then, I wouldn't have to deal with this until tomorrow.

It didn't take long to hang the clothes back into the closet. The drawers took a little longer. He didn't bother putting everything back neatly folded. He could do that another time when he wasn't so tired. Nothing seemed to be missing. Even the small plastic case with the three silver dollars was still there.

Obviously, robbery was not the motive for the break-in.

There was nothing he could do about the broken lock. He put the heavy chair from the living room in front of the door. Not much to keep out an intruder, but it would make enough noise to wake him. Then he flopped into bed.

* * * *

He phoned Montana early in the morning, before she went to work and told her about his trip and the break-in.

"You want to file a police report?" she asked.

"No. It wouldn't do any good. I have a feeling this has something to do with Michael."

"Maybe they'll find some prints."

"I doubt it."

"What do you think they were looking for?"

"Whatever it is they didn't find it. Nothing seems to be missing."

"Don't shrug this off, Jeff. They could be back."

"I won't." He hesitated. Then he said, "You want to go out for supper Saturday night?"

She laughed into the phone. "Are you asking me out on a date?"

"Sure am. Pick you up at seven?"

"Okay."

Shortly after he hung up, the phone rang. "This is John Parker. Remember me? I'm Mr. Larkin's bodyguard. How are you?"

"Fine."

"Listen. Mr. Larkin was wondering if you want to bring over that stuff you mentioned. You know…those pictures and the journal. He wouldn't mind looking at them. Maybe he can help you out finding some answers. He cared about Michael very much and he is as anxious as you to find his killers. We Ten Commandos look out for each other."

"That's kind of him, but something has come up. A new lead. I may be solving the mystery of the key. If I need help I certainly will call on you. Thanks."

When he hung up, he wondered why Larkin was so interested.

Anxious to find out what was in that deposit box he drove to the bank right after breakfast. Since it wasn't registered under his name, the clerk was reluctant to give him access to it, but when he explained that his brother was dead and showed her his badge, she shrugged.

"I guess it's all right. Normally I shouldn't do it without a death certificate and proof of Power of Attorney, but since you're a cop, I'll make an exception."

Inside the box was nothing but an envelope containing an SD card, another key, and a note saying McGee has the rest.

He remembered Dennis Kim telling him that McGee saw it all. Whatever it was that he saw.

He didn't have a card reader on his computer to download the SD card or to view it, but he knew that the girls had all the necessary hardware and software on their computer. He just had to wait until Sunday. Of course, the other option would be to go to the office and use the police computer, but he decided against that in case the SD card contained sensitive material.

In the afternoon, he made a call to someone from his past. "Hello, Colonel," he said, "this is Jeff Chartrand."

"Hello, Lieutenant Chartrand." The voice of Colonel Cowley still sounded as gruffly as he remembered. "I expected your call."

"You did?"

"Yes, I did. Where are you calling from?"

"From a phone booth a couple of blocks from my residence."

"Good. I see you haven't lost your touch." The Colonel allowed himself a small chuckle. Then his voice turned serious. "I'm sorry about your loss, Lieutenant. Your brother was a good soldier."

"Yes, he was, that's probably what got him killed."

"What do you know about it?"

"Nothing, really, nothing but suspicions. Can I come in?"

"When?"

"Today."

"I'll send someone. Ask him if he's thirsty."

"I'll be waiting."

The man who picked him up didn't look older than twenty, but Jeff wondered about that. The way he dressed and acted made him look young and harmless. Jeff wasn't fooled by that. Nobody working for Grey Ops was harmless. When he knocked on the door to Jeff's apartment, Jeff let him in and said, "Are you thirsty?"

"Thanks, I already drank in the office," he said.

Jeff smiled. The past sixteen years seemed to fall away as if they never happened and, for a moment, he was back in the Service. "When it comes to passwords you guys still don't have much imagination," he said.

The young man returned his smile. "The Colonel thought it would make you feel at ease. We have better ways now to recognize each other." He looked around the apartment. "Want me to sweep the place?" He didn't wait for Jeff to answer and produced a small device, which he held in front of him. Then he walked over to one of the table lamps, lifted it up and removed a tiny flat circle from its bottom.

"Not very original." He looked at Jeff's answering machine. Putting his finger on his lips, he moved his device over it. With a satisfied grunt, he peeled off a tiny sliver from one of the sides. Taking a small metal box out of his pocket, he dropped the sliver into it. "I guess the lamp was a diversion." He looked at Jeff. "How long have they had you under surveillance?"

Jeff shrugged. "I had a break-in yesterday. But this could have been here for a while."

"By the way, I'm Rob."

"I'm Jeff." He held out a hand.

Rob shook it. "I know who you are, Lieutenant. The Colonel speaks highly of you. You're a bit of a legend in the Corporation. I'm pleased to meet you. If you're ready, let's go."

They drove in silence in the young man's car. A Volkswagen beetle. At least it was a fairly new model. Rob kept looking in his rear-view mirror, and once he drove into a dark alley, waited for a moment, then he continued. Jeff didn't ask him to explain. Perhaps Rob was doing it only to impress him. His memory took him back to a time when he had done stuff like that.

Working for Grey Ops did that to you. Everything and everyone was treated with suspicion. Sometimes it was the only way to survive another day. He didn't know if they had been followed, he had seen no signs of it, but that didn't mean anything.

He glanced at a small screen on the dashboard. It looked like a GPS, but Jeff had a suspicion it was more than that. Times were different now. The gadgets available to the Military and Government were unknown to the civilian populace. For all he knew someone tracked them right now over a satellite system and knew his whereabouts anyway, regardless of the precautions his new companion took.

It didn't really matter. Not now. He was looking forward to his meeting with Colonel Cowley with uncertainty, not knowing if he could be of any help at all or if this whole thing might even be a mistake.

Rob drove his car into an underground parking lot. Then they took an elevator up to the eighteenth floor of the building they were in. The sign on the door read JC Exports and Imports.

The Colonel hadn't changed much. Sixteen years older, his hair gray, but he still looked good and as imposing as ever. His voice seemed a little rougher, and when Jeff looked into his eyes, he saw the wariness in the older man.

"Life as a civilian seems to agree with you," Colonel Cowley said. "I've missed you, though. You should have stayed with Grey Ops." He smiled. "You may be sitting in this chair now."

"I'm not sure if I would have wanted to," Jeff said. "It's a big chair to fill."

Colonel Cowley bent forward. "I read the papers and I know what they're saying. Too bad the media always makes a circus out of everything and fabricates these lies. What's this thing about drugs?"

"They found cocaine and cash in my brother's house. My brother never took drugs or pushed them. It is obvious, whoever killed him and his family left it behind to implicate him. They were looking for something but I haven't found out what. I'm afraid they'll be coming after my sister's family and possibly after me." Jeff gave the Colonel a rueful smile. "I'm a cop, but I can't protect them. I need to find out who is behind all this. That's why I need your help. I need your resources. I have a feeling something big is about to happen. My brother somehow knew about it and he needed to be shut up. Other members of his unit have been either murdered or attacked."

"You'll have to give us everything you've uncovered so far, Lieutenant Chartrand. I'll have my staff evaluate the information and then we'll see if we can help you. In the meantime, I would like you to connect yourself to our surveillance network. For your own safety." He gave Jeff a thoughtful look. "Anytime you want to come back and work for us, the offer still stands. You might want to give it some thought. I have a feeling you have stumbled into something you may not be able to handle by yourself."

Chapter Eleven

Montana didn't wear the red dress for dinner; instead, she had opted for a pair of tight white slacks and a light-blue jacket. The slacks were tight enough to show off her full buttocks and to make Jeff suspect she didn't wear any panties. The blouse she wore under the jacket revealed plenty of cleavage.

"Maybe I should skip the main course and go right for the dessert?" he joked and gave her a leering stare.

"Who said there'd be dessert?" She smiled coyly, and then she walked ahead of him toward the reserved table. He feasted his eyes on the seductive movement of her hips, obviously a little exaggerated, since she knew he was watching her.

How could I not have noticed her? Together for two years, every day, and I never saw the woman in her. To me she was just another cop.

After they were seated, she said, "I hear you went back to work yesterday."

"You heard correctly. How'd you find out?"

"Oh, I have my sources. Are you forgetting I'm a detective?"

"I guess I can't keep any secrets from you."

She reached across the table to touch his hand. "But you are. Is there something you're not telling me? Why would anyone break into your apartment? There had to be a reason. Stoneman acted a little peculiar today. I saw two guys in black suits in his office. They had Feds written all over them. I wonder what they wanted."

"I have a suspicion it has something to do with Michael's murder," Jeff said. "I went to Michael's bank and picked up an SD card."

"You never told me. What's on it?"

"I don't know. I'll go to my sister's place tomorrow and have the girls download it for me. I hope that I'll find something on it that will shed some light on this whole affair. It must be important. Why else did Michael and his buddies go to all this trouble to hide it? Who were they hiding it from?"

After they finished eating and Montana sipped on her fourth glass of Sauvignon Blanc, she leaned forward and said, "I'm ready for dessert. Tomorrow is Sunday. We can sleep in."

On the way to Jeff's place he suddenly said, "This is a little embarrassing, but I'd better stop at a drugstore."

She smiled. "Good idea. I don't have much faith in these feminine foams or the after douche."

He was familiar with this street and knew a drugstore was just ahead. Pulling up to the curb, he said with a sheepish grin, "Be right back," and got out of the car. He felt foolish buying condoms, especially when the young man behind the counter gave him a knowing smile.

Stepping out of the drugstore, he noticed the car parked on the other side of the street but didn't pay it much attention. A tall guy got out of it as Jeff walked around the front of his own vehicle. Something in the man's behavior or just plain instinct made Jeff look at him. When he saw what appeared like a gun in the stranger's hand, he froze.

"Hey there," the man shouted, "Is your name Chartrand?"

"Who wants to know?" Jeff asked, watching the hand with the gun.

"I have a message for you!" The gun came up.

Only sheer reflexes saved Jeff's life. The bullet that was meant for him whistled over his head and buried itself in a tree on the boulevard behind him. He heard the dull pfft as it penetrated the soft bark.

His own gun came out smoothly as he rolled away from the spot he had been standing on and from a lying position he returned fire. His bullet hit the man in the chest, the impact throwing him backward. He staggered, his body buckled and, almost in slow motion, he collapsed onto the hard concrete. Jeff rose, still wary. Gun still in hand and ready to be used again if necessary, he walked up to his assailant and kicked the gun out of the man's hand. Hearing the door of his car open, he knew that Montana was coming to his aid, and he also knew that she'd be scanning the surrounding area for other threats.

The man on the ground lifted his head and stared up at Jeff. "Why did you do it?" His voice sounded garbled like a man talking with his mouth full of water as red foam began to bubble around his lips.

"Why did I do what?" Jeff asked him, bending down to look into the man's face. He looked familiar.

"You didn't have to kill them." The voice came out weak.

"I didn't kill anyone," Jeff said. "Why were you trying to kill me?"

"They told me you murdered them." He coughed up blood and began to shake. "I just followed orders."

As the man's face slackened and his eyes glazed over, Jeff recognized him. His name was Ethan Grey. He was one of the Ten Commandos.

He stood up and said to Montana, "He's dead."

"I found this in the car," she said, holding up an attaché case.

"Let's check it out before we call it in." He looked at her. "You witnessed the shooting. It was self-defense. He fired the first shot."

She nodded. "Don't worry. You've got my back."

The door to the drugstore opened and the young clerk stuck out his head. "What's going on?" he yelled. "I heard gunshots."

Jeff flashed his badge. "Police. Everything is under control. Go back inside the store. For your own safety."

There was a streetlight right by their car. Jeff put the briefcase on the hood of the car and opened it. "What the hell!" He cursed when he saw his own face looking up at him from a stack of other pictures. The next pictures were of Dennis Kim and Toby Miller. Then Michael, Ronald Larkin, and John Parker. He also found a list of names and addresses.

"I believe we found our assassin," Montana said.

"I'm not so sure. This doesn't make any sense. This is Ethan Grey. He was in my brother's unit. Why would he want to kill his friends? And why me?"

"Maybe you'll find the clues on that SD card." Montana closed the case. "What do you want to do with this evidence?"

"Put it back into his car. We can't take it with us, since we're involved in the shooting. Let's call it in."

She looked at him. "This is not the way I intended to end this evening, but I'm afraid you went into the drugstore for nothing."

He gave her a rueful smile and nodded. "I guess the moment is gone."

Touching his cheek, she said, "There'll be others."

He drove her home and went back to his own apartment. Since sleeping was out of the question, he turned on the television. Flipping channels, he stopped at one when he recognized a familiar face.

Ronald Larkin. The would-be-senator and Michael's ex-commander.

"Mr. Larkin. What will be your priorities when you make it to the Senate?" The interviewer looked expectantly at the man in the guest chair.

Larkin smiled broadly at the reporter. "Thank you, Larry, for using the word when. I appreciate positive thinking." He turned toward the camera, his smile conveying confidence and sincerity.

Jeff had to admit, with his handsome looks Larkin gave the impression of a likable man. He would get votes based solely on his charismatic appearance.

"There are many issues that need to be dealt with. One, of course, is the housing crisis. Many Americans are faced with losing their homes, and they need help desperately. We need to lower interest rates or give homeowners some kind of tax credit. Secondly, I say we'll have to take a tougher stance with illegal immigrants. Tighten up the borders, for one thing. Illegal immigrants pose a great threat to our country. Terrorists could hide among them undetected." Larkin's handsome face showed concern and genuine conviction that he was the man to deal with the problems.

"It seems the safety of our country is one of your main issues, Mr. Larkin. Could you elaborate more on your thoughts about illegal immigrants?"

"Certainly. Every person residing in the United States of America needs to be either a citizen or a visitor. The whereabouts of anyone in our country should be known at all times. Illegal immigrants are not registered anywhere. We don't know who and where they are."

Larkin leaned forward and looked intently into the camera. "Let me make one thing clear. I'm not talking about Mexican Illegals. Certainly, they need to be registered and have their green card if they want to work here, but I don't think they pose a threat to our national security. I'm talking specifically about people from the Middle East, who might be coming into the States from our northern borders, for instance."

"You mean Canada?"

"Well, yes. I'm not saying that Canada harbors terrorists, but let's face it, Canada's immigration policies are not as stringent as ours. Canada has a large Muslim community. I'm also talking about visitors whose visas have expired. They might be hiding among the general populace for years, posing as American citizens. We have to flush them out. If we don't, I can see another terrorist attack on the horizon, larger than the one on September 11, 2001."

"Are you making a prediction, Mr. Larkin?"

Larkin smiled. "No, I'm predicting nothing. I'm saying we need to protect our country against such a possibility."

"You have done active duty in Iraq. As a war veteran what is your opinion on the continued occupation of Iraq? Many Americans disapprove of the way the current administration handles this war."

"It is something that needs to be addressed. I'd like to skip that subject, if you don't mind."

"One more thing. What are your thoughts on Iran? Senator Osborne thinks we should invade Iran. Do you agree?"

"I don't necessarily agree, but neither do I disagree. I'd say we should keep an open mind."

"Thank you, Mr. Larkin."

Jeff switched off the television. Larkin had made some valid points. How much he would be able to accomplish without support was another question.

* * * *

When Jeff arrived at the precinct Monday morning, Lieutenant Beacher called him into his office. Two men in dark suits watched him walking in. He couldn't see their eyes behind their sunglasses, but he knew they were studying him.

"I heard you were involved in a shooting Saturday night," Beacher said.

"That's correct," Jeff answered. "Someone tried to kill me."

Beacher didn't comment. He turned and indicated the two men in the chairs. "These are agents MacKay and Manning from Homeland Security. They would like to have a word with you."

Jeff looked at the men and asked, "Why?"

"We don't need a reason," the one with the mustache said.

"You guys may be Homeland Security," Jeff said belligerently, "but you'll need a valid reason to question me. You tell me why you want to talk to me or I'm not talking. I know my rights."

"When it comes to the security of our country you forfeit all your rights, Chartrand," the other agent growled. He looked at Beacher. "Leave us alone, Lieutenant. We'll take it from here."

"Take my advice, Chartrand. Cooperate with these guys," Beacher said in a low voice. Then he left.

The agent who had told Beacher to leave walked behind the desk and sat down. "Have a seat, Chartrand."

Jeff took one of the chairs. The agent with the mustache took up position behind him.

"Just for the record. Your name is Jeff Chartrand, is that correct?"

"Detective Chartrand to you, Lieutenant MacKay."

The agent gave him a sharp stare. "How do you know my name?"

"Lieutenant Beacher introduced you."

"He only gave you our names but never pointed us out."

"You served with my brother in Iraq. You were one of the Ten Commandos. I recognize you from my brother's pictures."

"You and your brother talked a lot about his time in Iraq?"

"We talked."

"What did you talk about?"

Jeff chuckled. "What is this? Twenty questions? It's none of your business what my brother and I discussed."

"Everything you and your brother discussed is our business. Just for your information, my name is not John, it's Dave. I'm his twin brother. John is dead. He died under very mysterious circumstances in Iraq. Michael never mentioned that?"

"No he didn't. I'm sorry to hear about your brother."

"How long have you had ties to the Muslim community?" Manning, the agent beside him, asked with a sharp voice.

The question came unexpected. "What the hell does that mean?" Jeff turned his head to look at the agent.

"We're the one asking the questions, not you, Chartrand!" Manning said. "Just answer my question."

"If you want answers then you better ask the right questions, Agent Manning. What reasons would I have to be involved with a Muslim community?"

"You tell us. We know your brother paid money to an international organization funded by terrorists, namely the Al Qaeda." Manning bent close to his ear. "Don't deny that you went to the mosque on thirty-fourth last Monday morning. We know you were there."

"That was the first time I ever saw the place." Jeff turned his head again and gave the agent a penetrating stare. "Are you keeping me under surveillance?"

"Why did you go there?" MacKay asked from the other side of the desk.

"To find out answers to the question you're asking. I think we're done here. You've got nothing on me." Jeff tried to rise, but Manning pushed him back into the seat. "We're done when we say so, Chartrand."

"Your brother had a journal. We understand it is in your possession," MacKay said.

"Are you using some kind of interrogation tactics on me?" Jeff smiled grimly. "Let me give you some advice…you're wasting your time. It won't work on me."

"Just answer the question!"

"Who told you I had my brother's journal?"

"Dennis Kim told us. Do you have it?"

"No. I haven't been able to get into my brother's house to look around."

"Maybe he kept it somewhere else?"

Jeff shrugged. "I wouldn't know." He wasn't going to tell these two clowns anything about the journal. "What's in the journal that might interest you?" he asked.

"We won't know until we see the journal," MacKay said. His eyes bored into Jeff's. "Did your brother ever show you pictures?"

"What kind of pictures?"

"Pictures he took with his camera."

"Yes, he did."

"What was on those pictures?"

"They were pictures from Iraq. Pictures of the guys in his unit…and others."

"Anything unusual about any of them?"

"If you call pictures of Iraq's countryside unusual, then I guess they were. Not really unusual, just interesting."

MacKay was still staring at him. "Your brother had a digital camera. Did he ever talk to you about a certain SD card he might have had in his possession?"

Jeff frowned and bent forward. "Listen, I have no idea what exactly you're fishing for. All I can tell you is yes Michael showed me a bunch of pictures from Iraq and his time there. I saw nothing unusual in any of them. I know nothing about an SD card. Obviously, he had one in his camera. He probably deleted the pictures he took and used it again to take more pictures. Maybe from his son's birthday. I don't know. What more can I say?"

"You shot a man while involved in a shootout Saturday night." Agent Manning changed the subject without leading into it.

"Your information is correct," Jeff said, puzzled by this question, wondering where it would lead.

"You killed this man, a former soldier, who served with your brother in Iraq. His name was Ethan Grey," MacKay said. "He was a member of my brother's and your brother's unit."

"He tried to kill me. I shot him in self-defense."

"So you say. That is still to be determined."

"My partner Maxine Montana witnessed the shooting."

MacKay chuckled. "You're sleeping with her. She is biased, and that makes her an unreliable witness. As far as we know she might even be your accomplice."

"You are keeping me under surveillance. I would like to know why," Jeff said angrily. "Just for your information, but you probably know this already, Ethan Grey had a list of names with him. He might very well be the man who murdered my brother."

"You believe that?"

"No."

"Then why are you implicating him? Did you know that Ethan Grey spent his last year in an asylum?"

"I didn't know that."

"I guess you don't know either that a man who fits your description signed your name on the weekend pass that allowed Ethan Grey to leave the asylum?"

Jeff sat up straight, startled. "What? Are you saying I released that man? I don't even know him, except from pictures my brother showed me. Why would I do that?"

"Have you checked your bank account lately?"

Jeff shook his head. This line of questioning was finally getting to him. "Where are you going with this?"

Manning produced a piece of paper. It looked like a printout of a bank account. Jeff stared at it, noticing the balance of 125,385.47 dollars.

"Look at the names at the top."

He did. Michael Chartrand. The second name was his. "I know nothing about this account," he said.

"That is your name, isn't it? Look at the last entry. Somebody deposited twenty thousand dollars a few days before your brother and his family was murdered. We had it traced. It came from a bank in the Cayman Islands. Who sent you this money and why?"

"That's not my account," Jeff said stubbornly, irritated by the agent's smug attitude. "As far as I know you created this piece of garbage to throw me off. Anyone can print something like this on a computer. This proves nothing. I'm telling you again, I don't know anything about a large sum of money deposited into any of my accounts. If what you're showing me is real, then a mistake has been made."

MacKay leaned back in his chair. He smiled, reminding Jeff of the Cheshire cat from Alice in Wonderland. He expected the agent to disappear at any moment. It would have been a great relief, like waking up from a nightmare. "A mistake? Very convenient and terribly coincidental."

Jeff rose in his chair. When Manning tried to push him back down, he kicked back with his elbow, registered with satisfaction the whoosh of air from the agent's lungs. He saw MacKay go for his gun and pointed a finger at him. "Don't do anything you may regret. Just for your information, I've been a bit paranoid lately, so I got myself one of those tiny transmitters. Everything that was said in here has been recorded, and I'm not telling you guys where the receiver is located and who has it, but if anything happens to me, it will be on record somewhere." He smiled.

"Just a little bit of insurance. One never knows when it comes in handy, right? I'm sure you guys have your own gadgets."

"Don't be stupid, Chartrand," MacKay said. "If you had a transmitter we would have picked it up. Like you said, we have our own gadgets, military stuff, and they're superior to anything you can get as a civilian. You're bluffing." He looked at Manning. "Frisk him."

Jeff had moved out of his chair. He glared at Manning. "Don't even try unless you want your fucking arm broken. I'm going to walk out of here now and you won't stop me. If you want to talk to me again, you get a court order from a judge, or produce evidence that I've committed a felony."

"You've got it wrong, Chartrand," MacKay said softly, "We don't need a court order or evidence to hold you or question you. We are…"

"I know who you are," Jeff interrupted him coldly. "You're from Homeland Security and you think you have the power to do whatever you wish. Go ahead, shoot me and find out that you are wrong. Someone will question you and you'll spend the rest of your life in some dark rat hole." He turned and walked out of the door.

Lieutenant Beacher intercepted him as walked to his desk. "What the hell happened in there?"

"Nothing. I think I made a mistake coming in today. If you don't mind, I'll take the rest of the day off."

He didn't make it out of the door. Two men in suits came up to him as he walked away from his desk. "Jeff Chartrand?" One of them said.

"Yes."

"Internal affairs. Leave your gun and badge, you're coming with us."

* * * *

Montana didn't look happy after he told her about his suspension. "Sorry to hear about that. It was a clean shoot. I told them so. How long?"

Jeff lifted his shoulders. "Who knows? It could be for a long time. Those guys from Internal Affairs acted under orders from someone else."

"What are you going to do?"

"Find out who murdered Michael and Samantha. And little Joseph. Now more than ever I'm determined to find those bastards. Maybe my suspension is a good thing. It'll give me the time and freedom I need."

He hesitated, didn't know if he should tell her. "There is something else. I never told you much about my past, when I was in the Military."

"I know you were in the Military Police."

"I was, but actually it was Army Intelligence, a special branch of Army Intelligence. They've expressed an interest in recruiting me again. I might just take them up on it."

"Why are you telling me this?" She gave him a long look.

"I want you to know. There should be no secrets between us. Just don't tell anyone about this, okay? If the wrong people find out what you know about me, your life might be in danger. What we did in Grey Ops was not always exactly…ah…above board."

"You mean it was outside the law?"

He looked at her and smiled grimly. "Forget we had this conversation. Just don't worry about me, that's all."

She moved close to him and kissed him. "Be careful, Jeff. I…I love you."

He stroked her hair, not sure how he should respond. He was very much attracted to her, but did he love her? They had sex. Once. Would have had again if not for that unfortunate incident with Ethan Grey, but that didn't mean that they were lovers.

He thought of Connie, a woman he had met only a short time ago. Different from Maxine in many ways; in appearance and demeanor sensuous and terribly exciting with her exotic looks. They had made love twice, and he suddenly realized he wanted to see her again.

Smiling at Montana, he pulled her close and held her. "I'll be fine," he whispered into her ear.

"I want you to be safe, not just fine." She pressed herself against him. "I'm not sure how often we can see each other. I've been…advised not to stay in contact with you."

"Advised? By whom?"

"Homeland Security."

"Those bastards!" Jeff cursed. "I don't trust them, especially not that MacKay. There is something about him that makes me question his motives. I can't put my finger on it."

Her arms went around his neck. "Make love to me now, Jeff. I need to feel you, touch you." She pulled him toward her bedroom, smiling. "Please, stay the night."

Chapter Twelve

Barbara was visibly upset. "Jeff, how long is this going to go on? I'm afraid to set foot out of my door. Now I can't even go shopping anymore without being accosted."

"Hold it. Start from the beginning. Who accosted you?"

"Two men. In the parking lot of Miller's Food Mart. They asked about you. Wanted to know where you could be found. I told them in the phone book."

"What did these men look like?"

"They looked like foreigners. They had beards and spoke with a heavy accent. I think they were from the Middle East." She stared at him. "What was Michael involved in, Jeff?"

He shrugged. "I don't know, sis. I really don't." He studied his empty glass of whisky, tempted to ask Barbara for another shot. Lately, he'd been drinking more than usual. Looking around his sister's living room, he felt a stab of envy. She had a nice house, a good husband, and three teenage girls to look after. She led a normal life.

He corrected himself.

Had lived a normal life. Until this thing happened with Michael.

She poured whiskey into her own glass. He had never seen her drink hard liqueur before. "Want another one?" she asked.

"Sure, why not." He heard the girls giggling in the basement room. At least they seemed to have adjusted well. "How's Angie doing?" he asked.

"She's doing fine," Barbara said. "I think living with us has helped her a lot." Her dark eyes studied him. "What's going on, Jeff? I hear you've been suspended. Why?"

He shrugged. "I shot a man. In self-defense. After he tried to kill me." He didn't tell her that the man's name was Ethan Grey, and that he had been one of Michael's war-buddies.

"You should have listened to Mom and become an accountant, like Helmut, or taken over the farm, the way Dad wanted, but no, you had to become a cop." Her eyes and expression showed the fear she felt. She reached out and touched his cheek. "I don't want to loose you, too, Jeffrey. Losing one brother is enough."

"Don't worry, Barb. Nothing is going to happen to me. Speaking of Helmut, where is he?"

"He had to go to the airport and pick up an old friend who flew in from Germany. He'll be staying with us for a couple of days."

"I didn't know that. You never mentioned it when I called."

"I forgot. I guess that incident with those two men bothered me too much." She rose. "I'd better check on the roast in the oven. You'll stay for supper, won't you?"

Jeff nodded and smiled. "If I'm invited. I haven't had a good home-cooked meal for ages."

"You should have married again. A man shouldn't live alone. He turns weird," Barbara said.

"Michael told me that already. More than once." He watched her walking into the kitchen. Tall, dark-haired, a beautiful woman of thirty-three, and yet, he still thought of her as his baby-sister; ten years old, scrawny, tall for her age, with large dark eyes; compliments of their Sioux grandmother.

She came back a few minutes later and brought him a beer. He smiled when he looked at the label. "Helmut still doesn't like our American beer, I guess?"

Barbara chuckled. "It won't happen. Not in this lifetime." She turned to walk back into the kitchen. "I'll be busy for a bit. Maybe you want to watch some TV?"

"Not really, but I wouldn't mind if I could use the girls' computer. I have an SD card and I want to check it out."

"Did you buy a digital camera?"

"No. The card belongs to someone else." He didn't want her to know it belonged to Michael. She had plenty of stuff on her mind already; no need to give her more things to worry about.

"The girls are in the basement. Just go down and ask them to help you."

He sniffed the air before he went downstairs. "Smells good," he said. "Brings back memories of Mom's Sunday dinners."

The girls were playing some kind of board game. A warm feeling touched his heart when he saw Michelle's pretty face and heard her cheerful laughter. She was only eleven, but it was evident she'd be a beautiful woman some day, like her mother. She had Nicole's auburn hair and green eyes. And her long legs.

She looked up when Jeff came down the stairs and smiled at him. "Hi, Jeff," she said.

"Hi, Michelle." Looking at the other girls, he said, "Hi, Mandy. Hi, Angie. Can I interrupt your game for a moment? I have a SD card I'd like to download into your computer. There's some stuff on it I want to check out."

"I'll do it," Michelle said. She giggled. "These two have no clue what to do."

"We do so," both girls protested.

"This is my job," Michelle told them. "Because Jeff is my father and he needs me." Her green eyes studied his face. "Right, Jeff?"

He smiled, a lump suddenly forming in his throat. She had called him my father, something she had never done before. "Yes, I need you," he said softly.

She inserted the little chip into the slot in the computer and waited for it to download.

"Do you mind if I look at it by myself, Sweetheart? This is police business, you understand?"

"I understand," she said, smiling knowingly. "Secret stuff, huh?"

"Very. I'll let you know when I'm done. Okay?"

"Okay."

He clicked on the file to open it. A score of pictures began to take shape on the screen. Jeff scrolled through them quickly and noticed some were not pictures but short videos. When he began to study the individual pictures, he didn't know what to make of them at first. They showed soldiers in battle gear. American soldiers. Some pictures showed Iraqi civilians. Mostly men.

Then suddenly he saw a sequence. A series of pictures showed an assault on a building. A hospital by the looks of it.

Then he stared at the pictures of the casualties of the assault. He cursed silently when he saw mostly dead women and children. Something obviously had gone wrong here.

Another series of pictures showed men, Iraqis, he assumed, were unloading crates from US Military trucks. American soldiers supervised the operation. Unfortunately, the pictures were not clear enough to make out any faces.

When he watched one of the short videos, he wanted to curse and smash his fist into the screen, because there was no mistaking what the video had captured.

The raping of a woman.

An Iraqi woman.

A soldier, clearly an American, hit her across the face. Then he stripped her naked and threw her to the ground. Another soldier dropped between her legs, forced open her thighs and began raping her.

Both soldiers had their faces turned away from the camera.

"Son of a bitch!" Jeff moaned. Could this be the reason Michael had been murdered?

The next video shocked him even more. The same naked girl lay on the floor, looking up at a soldier standing above her. The expression on her face showed anguish and fear. The soldier pulled out his sidearm, aimed it at the girl's head and shot her.

Her body kicked and then lay still. A pool of blood began forming around her head, soaked into the dirt, staining it dark, like a grotesque shadow.

Jeff closed his eyes, swallowed hard. This was the terrible thing Michael had carried with him since his return from Iraq. A secret that may have cost him his life. Who was the soldier raping the girl? And who shot and killed her?

Michael had known. So had Toby Miller. Both dead now. Obviously, Dennis Kim had been a witness to this, but did he still remember enough about it? He needed to talk to him again. Perhaps he had regained his memory.

He recalled Kim saying that McGee knows. Knows what? About Michael's journal? Or was he talking about this incident?

"Are you all right, Uncle Jeff?"

He looked up and stared at Angie, who stood on the other side of the monitor. "I'm fine," he told her.

"You look like you've seen a ghost or something."

He forced a smile. "Maybe I have." Closing the file, he pulled out the SD card and put it into the little plastic bag he used to protect it. "Do you know how to use this computer?"

"Of course I do, Uncle Jeff." She giggled. "Every kid knows how to use a computer. Only adults don't."

"Can you burn this file into a CD for me?"

"Sure. Just let me get a blank disk."

She inserted the disk and started the process of burning the file. He waited until it was done, then he deleted the file from the computer. This was information for certain eyes only.

"How about you people down there coming up for supper?" Barbara called from the top of the stairs. "Papa is home."

"We'll be up in a minute, Mom," Mandy called.

Jeff put the CD into his coat pocket and climbed up the stairs.

Helmut beamed at him and shook his hand. "Hallo, Schwager, how is it going with you?"

For an accountant Helmut had quite a strong grip. "I'm fine, Helmut." Jeff looked at the man with him. "This must be your friend from Germany."

"Ja, this is Werner Reinhart. He just came over from Frankfurt." Letting go of Jeff's hand, he said to his guest, "Werner, this is mine Schwager Jeff Chartrand. He's with the Polizei."

Reinhart shook Jeff's hand. He was a big man, as tall as Jeff but more massive. Blond and blue-eyed, he had this typical stereotype German look. A thin mustache adorned his upper lip, lending him a slightly old-fashioned appearance. "Pleased to make your acquaintance, Herr Chartrand," he said, his blue eyes sizing up Jeff. He sounded almost like an Englishman with his Oxford English, but his German accent still came through.

"Call him Jeff." Helmut laughed. "Remember, this is America. People here are more casual."

"I'm aware of that," Reinhart said. "But we don't really know each other." He peered intently into Jeff's face. "You look very familiar. Have we met somewhere before?"

Jeff shrugged. "I'm quite certain I've never seen you before and I have an excellent memory for names and faces, especially faces." He smiled faintly. "And I would surely remember yours."

"You're a policeman. I guess you would." He shook his head. "I have a good memory for faces also and I know I've seen you somewhere. It'll come to me."

"How about introducing me?"

"I am sorry, mine Schatz. Sometimes I forget my manners. Werner, this is my beautiful wife, Barbara."

Reinhart made a little bow. "Ahh, the Lady of the House. Helmut told me everything about you. I am honored to meet with you. You are even more beautiful than he explained to me."

Barbara laughed and looked at Helmut. "I like your friend already. I think he is a charmer." She stepped forward and held out her hand. "Welcome to our home, Mr. Reinhart."

He took her hand and held it briefly to his lips. "Thank you, Frau Helmann."

"Wow!" Barbara smiled. "You are a charmer, Herr Reinhart. Kinda old-fashioned, but I like it. I've only seen this in movies. I didn't know they still did this. I bet you even hold open the door for a woman."

"Of course I do." Reinhart chuckled. "But you are correct. Even in Germany, it is not the custom anymore. The American influence, you know, not that I'm saying it is a bad thing. Don't misunderstand me."

"There is nothing wrong with showing a woman a little respect. God knows we don't get much of it anymore these days." Barbara smiled at her husband. "That's why I love Helmut. He does have an old-fashioned streak in him." She brushed both of her hands on her apron. "Come, take off your coats. Maybe you want to freshen up a little before we eat?" Looking at Helmut, she whispered, "Don't take too long, Honey. I don't want the roast to get cold."

* * * *

"You are not only beautiful but also a good cook, Frau Helmann," Reinhart said. "Helmut is a lucky man."

"Well, you tell him that, Mr. Reinhart," Barbara said, "and please, stop calling me Frau Helmann. I'm Barbara to all of my friends."

"Okay, Barbara, but you must also call me Werner." Reinhart lifted his glass in a toast. "To good friends. Prost."

Jeff had been watching the man. He couldn't quite make up his mind if he liked Herr Werner Reinhart or not. He seemed jovial and educated. Well-mannered to the point of almost being absurd. Like a character out of a Humphrey Bogart movie. Sometimes his English sounded impeccable, at other times he seemed to search for the proper words.

"How do you two know each other?" Barbara asked, while reaching for the gravy bowl.

"Helmut and I went to school together," Reinhart said. "We were never really close friends, but we played in the same football team."

"You played football, Honey?" Barbara gave Helmut a surprised look.

"They call it soccer here," Helmut said. "In the Old Country soccer is called football, because you kick the ball with your feet, no touching with your hands."

"Well, you never told me you played soccer," Barbara chuckled. "What else are you hiding from me, Honey?"

"He was quite a good player, too," Reinhart said.

"You were much better, Werner." Helmut laughed good-humoredly. "You were better in everything, as I remember."

"Except in mathematic. You beat me there." Reinhart joined Helmut's laughter. "Anyway, prost to old times." He emptied his glass. "Good beer," he commented, "and served in a glass as it should be. American beer?"

Helmut chuckled. "I don't drink American beer. Only imports. From Germany."

"You live in America now, old Freund. You should drink American beer." Reinhart looked at Jeff. "Your last name, Chartrand. It is not an English name."

"It's French."

"You are French? Parlez vous francais?"

"No, I don't. I'm French by name only. Actually, I'm part Sioux, but I don't speak that language either. Just good old American."

"Sue?" Reinhart gave him a questioning look.

"Yes, Sioux. I've got Indian blood in me." Jeff smiled. "From my grandmother's side."

"Sue?" Reinhart repeated. "How do you spell that?"

"S-I-O-U-X."

"Aha, I understand. In Germany we say Zee-ooks. Wirklich? I am so excited to meet a real Indianer. When I was a boy, I read all the books by Karl May, books about the Old West. I loved Old Shatterhand and Winnetou, the Chief of the Indianer. In my country, we love Indianer. We find you people so…romantisch. Living on reservations, in tents. Living off the land. Hunting and fishing. I find that exciting."

"Not all Indians live on reservations, and the ones who live there don't find it very exciting, I'm sure. By the way, they don't live in tents anymore and they prefer to be called Native Americans." Jeff remembered his grandmother. She grew up on a reservation. He loved listening to her stories about her people. His people.

The history of the Sioux. Before the white man came to take away their land, their hunting grounds, their way of life. When the prairies teemed with buffalo, and when the tribes moved with the herds across the land.

Had that been romantic? Jeff didn't know. How romantic is it to live in a teepee, sitting around a smoking fire in the winter, sleeping cuddled inside a fur during those frigid temperatures? Melting snow for drinking water? Having no toilet paper?

He shuddered, just thinking about that.

No, thank you very much.

It might be fun doing it for a couple of weeks during a holiday in the wild backcountry, but then it was good to come back to civilization. The native population of America might have lived like that in the past, but this was the twenty-first century. Time doesn't stand still…things change, people change. You can't go back to the past. But, hell, who wants to? He had lived in near primitive conditions in 1991, while stationed in Kuwait. Except there had been no snow or bitter cold, only sand and blistering heat. It had not been romantic or exciting.

"I remember now where I saw you."

Jeff heard the voice of Reinhart, suddenly aware that his thoughts had drifted. "I'm sorry," he said, "I didn't pay attention."

"I remember where I know you from," Reinhart said. "I saw you in Iraq."

"I guess your memory isn't as good as you think." Jeff smiled. "I was never in Iraq."

"You are sure?" Reinhart squinted at him.

"I think I'd remember. Maybe you mean Kuwait? I was stationed there during the gulf war."

Reinhart shook his head, studying Jeff. "Your face is very familiar. Of course, you were dressed in army fatigues and you were younger, but I don't forget faces. It was Iraq."

"When were you in Iraq?" Jeff asked.

"In 2004."

Something suddenly clicked. "You're talking about my brother Michael," he said. "I look like him."

"You have a brother?" Reinhart leaned back in his chair and laughed. "I told you I remember faces. Where is he?"

"He's dead," Jeff said.

"Oh. Sorry to hear that. Did he die in Iraq?"

"No. He was murdered. Here. A few weeks ago." It surprised Jeff how easily he could talk about it.

"Murdered? How terrible." Reinhart glanced at Helmut. "You should have told me. You must all still be grieving. Maybe I should not have come here." He looked at Barbara. "I'm so sorry for your loss. It is a terrible thing to lose a loved member of the family. I know how you feel. I lost my sister a few years ago. I am still sad about it."

"Don't feel bad about coming here, Werner," Barbara said. "Maybe a diversion is good for us." Her eyes lingered on Angie for a moment, and then she said, "Angie is my brother's daughter. She lives with us now."

"That is good," Reinhart said, apparently lost for words.

"What did you do in Iraq, Werner?" Jeff asked, trying to change the subject.

"I was working for a German construction company."

"I see. What did you do? Are you an engineer or something?"

Reinhart smiled, his eyes still studying Jeff. "No, I was there as a security guard. I'm a mercenary. A gun for hire."

"Really? Interesting. What's your business here in the States?"

Reinhart chuckled. "Now you sound like one of those custom's officers. I am here for an interview with my future employer. I'll be going back to Iraq."

"How did you meet my brother?"

Reinhart shrugged. "I don't remember the occasion. I only remember faces, that's all."

The way he said it made Jeff suspect that he was lying. He knew exactly where he had met Michael. This man was a mercenary, a soldier with no loyalties. He might be German by birthright or choice it really didn't matter. He was true to only one country...the one his employer belonged to, and that loyalty could change at any time. This man was true to whoever paid him the most money.

The pictures from the SD card flashed across Jeff's mental screen. "Was the company you worked for in Iraq involved in the selling of weapons?" he asked bluntly.

Reinhart gave him a startled look, his eyes seemed suddenly cold and his face showed a wary expression. "Why do you ask? Did your brother tell you that?"

"No, but I saw pictures."

"I was in those pictures?"

"Not that I can recall. My brother never mentioned anything like that, either."

Reinhart let out a forced laugh. "You say you saw pictures of illegal arms dealings and you think I'm involved, but you have no proof that I was there when it happened. Is this some American joke I maybe don't understand?"

"No joke, I'm just curious. What did your company do in Iraq, Werner?"

"Road repairs. When you Americans bombed Baghdad you created a lot of work for people who are willing to get involved. Somebody is going to become rich building up that country again. I recognize an opportunity when I see it and I take advantage of it. Do you think that is a bad thing?" Reinhart spoke with a challenging voice.

"Someone always benefits from a war. There is a lot of money to be made right now selling weapons to the insurgents. Maybe your company decided to get in on the action. Might be more profitable than just building new roads."

"I'm sure someone is selling weapons. Not us." Reinhart pointed a finger at Jeff. "You know, you should be an interrogator. You are very good." He lifted his glass. "Prost, my Indian friend. I hope the people who murdered your brother get the punishment they deserve."

"I'll drink to that," Jeff said grimly. "And believe me, they will."

"Anyone for dessert?" Barbara asked.

"I'll have some," the three girls cried out in unison.

"Of course you do." Barbara laughed. "You don't even know what I made."

"If it's your famous cheesecake, I'll have a piece," Jeff said.

After dinner, they all moved into the living room, except for the girls, who went back into the basement.

"What made you become a mercenary?" Jeff asked. "Obviously, you must have served in the German army at one time."

"Ja, I did. I made it to second lieutenant. I couldn't rise any higher in the ranks because I don't have enough education. So I decided to quit and become a private agent." He laughed. "The pay is much more rewarding than what I could ever get in the army. Now I make more money than a General, even with my limited education. That is a joke, don't you find it?"

"It's also more dangerous, I would think."

Reinhart shrugged. "And more exciting. When my time comes to die, I can say I have lived."

"I'd rather die in my sleep," Helmut said. "Being an accountant is dangerous enough for me."

"Don't laugh," Barbara said when Jeff and Reinhart grinned. "These paper cuts he comes home with, unbelievable. One time he almost got his finger mangled in a paper shredder. That's my Helmut."

"We can't all be macho soldiers and cops," Helmut said, defending himself. "Another beer, Jeff?"

"No, thanks, Helmut. I'd better drive home. There's some stuff I want to check out and I'm getting up early tomorrow morning."

"I thought you weren't working anymore," Barbara said.

"I'll be driving to Fresno to talk to Dennis Kim again. Maybe he'll remember something." He was also thinking of Connie. Beautiful, exotic looking Connie. He couldn't get her out of his mind. Even without

Dennis Kim he might have taken a ride to Fresno just to see her. He longed for her company and her passionate embrace.

"Before you leave you must have at least one glass of Schnapps with us," Reinhart said. "I brought a bottle with me from Germany."

Jeff hesitated. The last thing he needed right now was to be picked up for driving while intoxicated, but then he shrugged. Germans seemed to have this thing about drinking Schnapps to bond with each other. He almost sputtered when he downed his glass. "How strong is this stuff?" he croaked, gasping for air.

"Good stuff, ja?" Reinhart laughed and slapped him on the back. "Puts hair on your chest…isn't that an American saying? Want another one? You can't stand on one leg."

Jeff lifted both hands and shook his head. "One is enough, thank you. I don't usually drink hard liqueur."

Barbara walked with him to the door and gave him a hug. "I don't have to tell you to be careful but I'm saying it anyway. We all want to find the killers, but I don't want you to put yourself in unnecessary danger, Jeff. I couldn't bear to lose you too."

He stroked her hair. "Don't worry, sis, I'll be careful." He saw her moist eyes and gave her a kiss on the cheek. "I love you and I'll do everything to protect you and the girls, I promise. I'll look into the incidence in the parking lot. We'll find out who those guys are."

She nodded. "Promise me you'll be careful."

When he drove home, he chided himself for having that last drink. He wasn't drunk, but he knew his blood alcohol was over the legal limit. His thoughts swirled around Werner Reinhart. A mercenary who came across as a good-humored kind of guy. With his overly German manners and polite talk it was easy to underestimate him and Jeff was not about to do that.

Something in the man bothered him. Jeff had no doubts he was involved in illegal ventures. Why would anybody in the States hire a German mercenary? There were plenty of ex-army veterans, or even former police officers, who were hiring out as security people for companies doing business in overseas countries.

What is your real reason for being here, Herr Reinhart?

Chapter Thirteen

Jeff decided to take the SD card and the CD with him to Fresno. Detective Smith was in his office when he arrived at the precinct. He showed great interest in the SD card and its contents. He downloaded it into his computer, and together they watched the video clips and studied the pictures.

"This is powerful stuff we're seeing here," Smith commented. "Problem is we don't know who these guys are. There are no faces. For all we know they could be a bunch of mercenaries wearing US army uniforms."

"I doubt that. They are US army but not necessarily anyone from Michael's unit. " Jeff said. "There is no question about the fact that the girl is being raped."

"And murdered in cold blood afterwards," Smith said.

"This is the kind of stuff that gives us Americans a bad name," Jeff said grimly.

"It seems we have found the reason your brother was murdered."

"It seems so but why after all this time? It's been three years since they're back from Iraq."

"What about all those other pictures? Clearly, someone was selling arms to insurgents." He looked at Jeff. "I hate to say it, but it appears your brother was involved in this. He's probably the man with the camera."

"It appears that way, doesn't it?" Jeff shook his head in denial. "There must have been a reason for this. Michael was not a traitor. I refuse to believe that. The fact that he kept these pictures proves he needed them for something. Maybe insurance? They were his trump card in a game he may not have wanted to play?"

"What about these images?" Smith pointed at the one with the dead civilians. "These are not soldiers. Insurgents? I doubt that. Too many women and children. Did a suicide bomber do this? Possible but highly unlikely. You are correct…there is a reason your brother kept these pictures and the video clips." Smith stared at Jeff. "You mentioned insurance. Your brother feared for his life, that's clear, just like Toby Miller and Dennis Kim. There is a connection between these murders after all."

"I'd like to question Dennis Kim again. Perhaps this will jog his memory."

Smith looked suddenly grave. He shook his head. "I'm afraid you're out of luck. Dennis Kim was shot to death in his hospital bed last night. The call came in at four this morning. That's when the nurse on duty found him."

"Shit!" Jeff curse loudly. "Any suspects?"

"None. Nobody saw or heard anything."

"I'm not surprised. We're not dealing here with local hoods or amateurs. Dennis Kim was assassinated, just like my brother and Toby Miller." Jeff stared at the computer screen. "I wish I could have talked to Kim. He might have been able to explain these pictures."

"Can I keep them on my computer?" Smith asked.

"Sure but don't broadcast to anyone that you have them," Jeff warned. "An attempt has already been made on my life. Somebody ransacked my apartment. I'm positive they were looking for this SD card."

"Now we just have to find out who wants it so desperately." Smith looked at Jeff. "I know we're working for different police departments, but perhaps we can work together on this. Exchange information as we discover it."

Jeff smiled grimly. "I never told you. I've been suspended."

"Why?"

"I was involved in a shooting. It was self-defense but Internal Affairs doesn't see it that way. You should also know that Homeland Security interrogated me."

Detective Smith whistled. "Homeland Security? You're involved in something big, my friend."

"You're sure you want to be part of this?"

Smith nodded. "You bet your ass, I do. Seems to me someone is trying to cover up something ugly. They may be looking for a fall guy. You need a friend badly. I assume that shooting had something to do with this case?"

Jeff nodded. "Ethan Grey, one of the Ten Commandos, tried to take me out. Someone hired him to do that."

"There are not many of them left," Smith mused. "Do you think one of the survivors is behind this?"

"It would be easy to assume that, but I wouldn't want to guess who? There are only four survivors. Larkin is running for Senate. His bodyguard, John Parker, is busy protecting him. I've met both of them. They didn't even know Michael was dead. That leaves McGee and Carrington. There was a note with the SD card, which said that McGee has the rest, whatever that is. Dennis Kim told us that already. Obviously, McGee is not behind it. James Carrington is the only other one left. Maybe I should talk to him next. There is only one problem. He lives in Minneapolis." He rose. "I'm going to see Connie Wu to express my condolence."

He left Smith with mixed feelings. This case was beginning to become more and more complicated.

Connie was in her apartment. "Sorry to hear about Dennis," he told her when she let him in.

"Now do you believe that Dennis was not the victim of a mugging?" she asked.

"I never believed he was, and neither did Detective Smith," he assured her and took her into his arms.

"I'm glad you came." She smiled. "I can use some company right now. Have you made any progress in your investigation?"

"Not really." He stroked her hair. "I've missed you." He kissed her gently and held her tight.

"I've missed you too. I was hoping you would come and visit me again."

Smiling, he looked into her almond eyes. "How could I not do that? I've been thinking about you all the time. You've bewitched me with your beauty and fiery passion."

"I have?" Laughing softly, she closed her eyes and pursed her lips. "Then kiss me again and kindle that fire inside me. Let's forget about Dennis, about your brother, and all our problems for a while."

She put a CD into the player. Then she began taking off her clothes, slowly removing each piece, like a stripper.

He sat in a chair and watched her, enjoying the way her body swayed to the soft music. Taking off her bra, she flung it at him, laughed when he caught it between his teeth. Then she came close, still wearing her lacy panties, she straddled him and pushed her breasts into his face.

"Lick them," she said.

He teased her nipples with his teeth, sucked one into his mouth. She moaned softly, wriggled her lower body. "I can feel you," she said, giggling.

Her hands undid the buttons on his shirt and slipped it over his shoulders. "You have hard muscles," she whispered.

He held her naked warm body against his, rose to his feet while she clung to him. Walking over to the couch, he laid her onto her back. He shoved his pants past his hips and didn't even bother to take off her panties, just pushed aside the crotch. Putting his hard penis between her labia, he slowly eased into her creamy sheath.

She moaned when she felt his manhood inside her, moved with him as he began rocking between her spread thighs. He took his time, enjoying the moments when she cried out in the grip of an orgasm.

"Let me take off my panties," she gasped.

"Okay," he said. While watching her as she slowly slipped out of her panties he undressed. When he moved back into the cradle of her clutching thighs, he sighed deeply. He rubbed his chest against her soft breasts, enjoying the way her smooth skin felt against his. She curled her fingers around his stiff member and moved her hand gently back and forth.

"Not like that," he groaned. "I want to come inside you."

"I wouldn't want it any other way," she moaned, guiding him into her creamy love canal. Snapping her hips back and forth, she reached her first orgasm almost immediately.

After supper, they went into the bedroom, where they spent most of the night exploring each other's bodies and experimenting with every position they could think of. He discovered Connie was quite supple and capable of doing things with her body not many women can do.

He left her early in the morning because he wanted to be home by noon, but he promised to be back for Dennis Kim's funeral.

* * * *

The drive home seemed to take longer than usual. He was tired but happy. He hadn't really accomplished much, except spending a wonderful and exciting night with Connie.

The bad news was that Dennis Kim was dead.

Murdered.

On the positive side, he had found an ally in Detective Smith, who shared his conspiracy theories after viewing the pictures and videos on the SD card. He was the only one. Even Maxine seemed to have her doubts.

Thinking of Maxine gave him pangs of guilt. He felt torn between Connie and Maxine. Connie, petite, dark-haired and lovely beyond description. Her oriental looks and flexible body made her exotic and desirable. She seemed to bring out his wild, passionate animal-side.

His feelings toward Maxine were just as strong. He loved her looks. Tall and blond, she had shown him a side of her he had never seen before. Cool and collected on the outside, her passion, when kindled, was as deep as Connie's. Their lovemaking had been different but no less exciting.

He suddenly realized something. When he thought of Maxine he didn't think of her as Montana, the way he used to do. Now it was Maxine.

What the hell have I gotten myself into? All these years of feeling lonely and now I can't make up my mind. Two beautiful women, both equally desirable, and both seem to be strongly attracted to me. I can't hurt either one of them, but eventually I will have to make a choice.

A feeling of deep regret followed him until he arrived at home.

A message on his answering machine told him to give 'your buddy Rob' a call. He started dialing Rob's number, but then he changed his mind; better to use the payphone in the laundry across the street. Even though Rob had swept his apartment for bugs, Jeff had suddenly become paranoid.

"Colonel Cowley wants to see you, Chartrand," Rob told him. "Don't use your car. Take the bus to forty-seventh and third. Someone will meet you there in two hours." Then he hung up.

Jeff smiled grimly. Sixteen years seemed to fall away like a cloak he'd been wearing. How easy it was to start playing the old games again...games of intrigue and mistrust.

Trust no one. Suspect everything and everyone. Don't become attached to anyone.

He shook his head. Did he want that again? He didn't, but he couldn't see a way out of it. Someone had tried to assassinate him once already. They would try again. He didn't expect any help from the law. He'd been suspended from his job. Homeland Security had him under surveillance. It was only a matter of days or at best a few weeks before he'd be arrested and charged with something, he was certain of that.

Damn you, Michael! What were you involved in?

He had a quick lunch in one of the small fast-food restaurants and then he boarded the bus. He would have preferred his car, but he knew he had no choice in the matter. That was the only way the Corporation worked.

He was supposed to transfer to another bus after about twenty minutes, but just before he stepped into the bus, someone touched his shoulder. When he turned, he saw Rob grinning up at him. "Change of plans," the young man said.

Jeff wasn't surprised. He followed Rob to his small car, which he had parked just around the corner.

"I hear you've been suspended," Rob said.

Jeff smiled grimly. "Bad news travels fast."

Rob grinned. "We like to be informed about the people who work for us."

"I'm not working for the Corporation. Not anymore."

"I know, but you will again." Rob glanced at him. "I'm looking forward to working with you, Lieutenant. By the way, we don't call it The Corporation anymore. We call it just Grey Ops." He smiled. "We don't actually exist officially, but you know that."

"Who says you'll be working with me?"

"I do." He shrugged. "You've been my hero ever since I joined Grey Ops. Even before that. My dad always spoke very highly of you. He's looking forward to having you back."

A suspicion began to form in Jeff's mind. "Who is your dad?"

"Colonel Cowley. Didn't you know?"

Jeff shook his head and sighed. "I didn't even know the Colonel was married."

"He isn't. My last name is not Cowley but Masters." Rob chuckled. "My dad knocked up my mom when he went to visit my grandparents. He and my mom were childhood sweethearts." He shrugged. "I guess it happens. He is human, you know."

A smile tugged on Jeff's lips. Damn! Who would have thought? "I would have never guessed," he said.

"That he is human or that he knocked up my mom?"

"Both." Jeff's smile turned into a grin. "That comes as a great surprise. When did you find out and when did the Colonel acknowledge you as his son?"

"Oh, I knew about him forever, but I never met him until I was eighteen. That's when he recruited me. Right out of College."

"How old are you, Rob?"

"Twenty-five."

"You look younger."

Rob sighed. "I know. I don't get the respect I deserve. I think I'll grow a mustache, or maybe a beard."

Jeff laughed. He was beginning to like this young man.

The Colonel sat behind his big desk, studying a file. He looked up and smiled when Jeff entered his office. "Glad you could make it, Lieutenant Chartrand. Sit down." He closed the file in his hand and put it into a drawer. Then he gave Jeff a thoughtful look. "You seem to be unemployed at the moment," he said.

Jeff smiled thinly. "Not unemployed, just suspended."

"Don't kid yourself, Chartrand. We both know that it is only a matter of time until you'll be dismissed from your job. Homeland Security will see to it." His eyes looked grave. "You've been put on the Watch list. Are you aware of that?"

"No but I'm not surprised. Seems I've stepped on somebody's toes or maybe I'm digging in an area where I'm not supposed to dig." He didn't ask the Colonel where he got his information. Grey Ops had spies in every branch of the government. Department of Homeland Security being one of them.

He remembered the SD card and pulled it out of his pocket. "I found this in my brother's stuff. You might be interested in it."

Colonel Cowley took it from him and inserted it into his computer, waited for it to download. Jeff didn't say anything, just watched the Colonel's face as he studied the images on his screen.

"Anyone else seen this?" Cowley asked after a while.

"A Detective Smith from the Fresno Police Department."

"Nobody else?"

Jeff shook his head.

"Who knows you have this?"

"I don't think anyone knows. The people who murdered my brother might believe I have it. That's assuming they know of the SD card's existence." Jeff shrugged. "Ronald Larkin, the guy who's running for Senate, knows I have Michael's journal, or part of it, and a key to a deposit box. His bodyguard, John Parker, also knows. I'm certain all the other guys in Michael's squad knew about it."

"Most of them are dead now, but there may be others," the Colonel said, his eyes on Jeff. "This won't stop until you're dead too. You'll have to make a decision. You cannot go this road alone. You need help." He leaned forward. "You can't expect any help from your department. By suspending you, they cut off your access to information. Your friend Detective Smith does not have the resources to find out anything of value. He'll be shut up if he starts digging. You have only one choice."

Jeff sighed and nodded. "You may be right."

"You know I'm right. We cannot help you unless you work for Grey Ops."

"What would I be doing?"

"I can't tell you until you make a decision." Cowley studied Jeff's face. "There is one thing I can tell you, though. I have a feeling your assignment will bring you a lot closer to finding out about your brother."

"How?"

"Make your decision and you'll know."

"I'll think about it, Colonel." Jeff rose. "Hang on to the SD card for me. I believe it'll be safer here than anywhere else." He still had the CD as insurance, should he need it.

"Don't think too long, Chartrand. I'm afraid time is running out. I'd hate to read about you in the obituaries."

Rob dropped him off at the same bus stop where he picked him up. He boarded the bus, settled into the seat and tried to sort out his thoughts. The Colonel was right. He needed the help and the recourses of Grey Ops. Alone, he was doomed to failure and his life expectancy not good. The best he could hope for was to be arrested on some trumped-up charge, but he didn't think that would happen. It was more likely the bullet of an assassin would find him. A bomb under his car could also do the trick.

Or maybe the next time he used his phone it would blow up in his face.

Damn it! Now he was really getting paranoid.

It began to rain the moment he stepped off the bus. When he walked past one of the fast-food places, he realized he was hungry, but not for a hot dog or hamburger. There was a nice Bar and Grill that served good food not far away from his apartment, within easy walking distance, but since it rained, he decided to go home and get his car. Looking at his watch, he noticed it was past five. Too late to drive to the bank to put the CD into his deposit box. Then he decided to take a quick shower, shave and change his clothing.

The phone rang when he was in the shower, but he let the answering machine pick it up. He heard a woman's voice, assumed it was Maxine. When he listened to the message after his shower, he discovered it wasn't Maxine but a woman who identified herself as Kalila Ahmed. She wanted to meet with him. She didn't leave a number.

Chapter Fourteen

It still rained when he pulled out of the underground garage. His wipers worked overtime to clear away the water pouring onto his windshield, and he had to switch on the fan to keep the inside from fogging up. Large puddles began to form on the street surface, and the few pedestrians hurrying down the sidewalk hugged the buildings to keep from being splashed by passing cars.

Ten minutes later, he was lucky to find an empty spot in the parking lot of the Silver Bar and Grill. The place was more crowded than usual, probably because of the rain, but he didn't have to wait long for a table.

Ordering a beer and a steak, he leaned back in his chair and relaxed. He should probably have phoned Maxine, even though she told him Homeland Security suggested she keep contact with him to a minimum.

She was a good cop and loved her job. He couldn't blame her if she kept her distance out of fear it might put her career in jeopardy. However, he'd be damned if he let some bastard like MacKay intimidate him. It didn't surprise him to find out he'd been put on a Watch list. Someone was out to get him. He needed to find out who.

Colonel Cowley made him an offer he had no choice but to accept.

When the waitress brought him his beer, he let it sit without taking a sip, just stared into the foam of the mug. Helmut would be happy in this place, since he preferred drinking his beer from a stein.

Wonder what his buddy Herr Reinhart is up to right now? Somehow, I have bad vibes about that man.

"Are you going to drink that beer or are you worshipping it?"

Startled, he looked up at the woman who had spoken. She gave him an amused look out of dark eyes. Smiling, she indicated the empty chair across from him. "Mind if I join you? All the seats are taken."

He didn't really feel like sharing his table, but then he shrugged. Something about her manner intrigued him. "Sure, why not?" he said, wondering why she chose him, especially since he saw a couple of empty chairs at other tables.

Before she sat down, she took off her jacket and draped it carefully across the back of the chair. He couldn't help but notice her slim body and the way her breasts strained against the material of her loose blouse.

"Is it not unpleasant weather?" she said, smiling at him across the table.

"It sure is." He watched her get comfortable in her chair.

She pulled out a small mirror from her purse and looked at herself. "I am always afraid my mascara might run when it gets wet, even though it is supposed to be waterproof," she said, laughing. Then she put her mirror away again, apparently satisfied with her appearance.

Her dark eyes studied him. "How is the food in this establishment?" she asked.

Even though her English was excellent, he detected an accent. That and her complexion and dark eyes made him wonder if she had been born in some other country than the States. "The food is good if you like American food," he said.

Her eyes widened for an instant. "Is it that obvious?"

"What?"

"That I am not American."

He smiled. "I'm just guessing. You have an accent, but that doesn't mean you can't be a citizen of this country."

"Well, I am not." Still looking at him, she said, "My name is Kalila Ahmed. I am the woman who left a message on your answering service."

Jeff took that first sip from his beer, speculating what she wanted from him. Suddenly, he felt apprehensive and on guard. "I guess I don't have to introduce myself," he said, putting down his mug. "Obviously, this isn't a chance-encounter."

"No, it is not. I followed you from your apartment."

"Why?"

"I wanted to meet you."

"Why?"

She chuckled softly. "Are you always this talkative?"

"Depends. You haven't answered my question." He looked at her sharply, wondering if she carried a gun in her purse.

"I have information you might be interested in, Mr. Chartrand."

He leaned forward, reached across the table and grabbed her wrist. "Before this conversation goes any further you'd better tell me who you are and how you know about me!"

"You are hurting me," she said.

"I'll hurt you more unless you start talking," he said harshly, getting tired of playing these cloak and dagger games. He took away his hand when the waitress came with his food. She looked at the woman. "Anything for you, ma'am?" she asked.

"Just a soft drink," Kalila said.

"Sure." The waitress looked at Jeff. "Anything else, sir?"

Jeff shook his head. "I'm fine, thank you. Can you bring me the bill? I'm somewhat in a hurry."

He watched the girl walking away and sighed. Only a short time ago he'd admired the play of her round buttocks inside her tight skirt and wondered if he should ask her out some day. In fact he had asked her for her phone number, which she refused to give to strangers. "Maybe if we knew each other a little better, I might give it to you," she told him, smiling. It seemed she didn't remember him.

How things had changed since then. His somewhat carefree life was gone, probably forever.

"I am a friend, Mr. Chartrand."

The woman's voice brought him back to the present. Staring into her dark eyes, he said, "Prove it to me by answering my question."

"Not here. I'd prefer a more private place."

He laughed. "Like my apartment, for instance?"

"No." She smiled. "My car. Or yours. Whatever you prefer."

"All right. Mine. After I finish my meal."

She watched him eat with a bemused smile. "You Americans," she said, "You have to have your steak and French Fries."

"You betcha," he said. "We Americans do a lot of things the rest of the world does not approve of, but we don't care. That's what makes us Americans and that's what makes this country so great."

"The Land of the Brave and Free," she said with a low voice. She couldn't quite hide the sarcasm. "I know all about that. How free are you really, Mr. Chartrand, when your own government tries to keep you from finding out who murdered your brother?"

"Who says it's the government that's behind it?" he countered. "I'm really curious to find out how you know so much about me and why."

She didn't answer, just gave him a cryptic smile.

He finished his meal, but he didn't enjoy it as much as he would have liked. Having a strange woman watching him eat didn't exactly add to the pleasure of eating a juicy steak and drinking a cold beer.

The rain had changed into a slight drizzle when they left the bar. He pulled up his collar to keep the wind from blowing the tiny drops of water down his neck.

"Nice car," Kalila commented when she slid into the passenger seat, rubbing her hands together to dry them. "Another thing you Americans love. Big cars."

Jeff shrugged. "The oil companies are trying their darnedest to make it nearly impossible for the average citizen to drive a big car. The way the price of gasoline is rising these days."

"As you said The oil companies! And do not forget the taxes your own country adds to the price of gasoline." She smiled, but it looked forced. "And everyone in the western worlds is, of course, blaming the Arab countries for the high cost of fuel."

"I'm not an economist and not informed enough to get into a discussion with you about who's at fault," Jeff said, giving her a hard look. "Now tell me, who are you and what do you want from me?"

He watched her closely as she opened her purse and pulled out an envelope. She handed it to him. "You might find this interesting and informative."

Taking the envelope from her, he opened it and shook out a stack of photographs. The first picture he looked at showed the image of a young dark-haired woman wearing a billowing black abaya. She wore headdress, but her face was uncovered. He recognized the face.

Kalila chuckled softly when he looked at her in surprise. "Where did you get this picture?"

"I took it with my camera. Go on and look at the others."

All of the pictures where of the same young woman. In a few of them, she held a little child in her arms.

The last picture made him hold his breath, but he had somehow expected it. He stared at Kalila, who had been watching him silently. "Who is this woman and how did you come into possession of my brother's picture?"

"I told you I took them. We have cameras where I come from."

"And where do you come from?"

"Why do you ask, Mr. Chartrand? You already know that, I am sure."

"Tell me anyway."

"I am a native of Iraq. To answer your other question, that woman in the picture is my sister."

"And the little boy?"

"He is my nephew. And yours. Your brother Michael's son."

Jeff stared at her in silence. Pieces of a puzzle were suddenly beginning to fall into place. He realized he had somehow suspected this all along. The first time he looked at the picture of Michael, the dark-haired young woman and the baby, a suspicion began to form in his mind, but he had tried to suppress the idea as absurd.

"Her name is Adira, and the boy's name is Omar."

"My brother paid money every month to one of the mosques. Was this money meant for her?"

Kalila nodded. "Yes. Your brother loved Adira and he loved his son."

"He was married for Christ sake," Jeff burst out. "He had a family here. A wife, a son and a daughter."

"I know, he made a mistake having an affair with my sister, but he was an honorable man. He tried to make things right."

"Where is Adira now?"

A dark cloud seemed to settle over Kalila's face. "She is dead."

"Dead? How?"

"Stoned to death by the people in the village she lived in. She committed an unforgivable sin. My people do not forgive sins like that."

"That is barbaric!" Jeff almost shouted it. He hated the fact Michael cheated on his wife, betrayed his family, and yet, this young woman did not deserve to be punished in such a horrible way. Visions of her covered in blood under a pile of stones thrown by a screaming mob flashed through his mind. "You people are not civilized. You don't deserve to be free!" he said between clenched teeth.

"Do not judge us by your standards, Mr. Chartrand. We have a different morality. We do not condone sex before marriage. We do not publish books, magazines and movies showing naked young girls having sex with a variety of men. We do not publish pornography on the internet."

"No, you probably don't," Jeff said sarcastically. "You'd rather show young American soldiers having their heads cut off by a butcher who is too cowardly to even show his face."

"Those atrocities are committed by fanatics, Islamic extremists, criminals, and not by the peace-loving citizens of Iraq." She spoke vehemently, her dark eyes flashed angrily. "If you Americans would pull out of Iraq and let us decide the fate of our own country, those incidents would stop. The insurgents would have no reason to kidnap foreigners and execute them."

"No, they'd come to our country and blow up a few more planes and buildings, killing innocent people on American soil." Jeff pushed the pictures back into the envelope. "Why are you showing me these? What you want from me? Money?"

"No. I wanted you to know about Adira and your brother's child. By the way, Omar is alive and living in an orphanage."

"In Iraq?"

"No. In Afghanistan. We managed to smuggle him out of the country. That orphanage is run by Canadians." Her eyes studied him. "I will not blame you if you want nothing to do with him. He is a beautiful boy. He has your brother's blue eyes."

Jeff put his head between his hands, his mind trying to digest the information. His brother had another son! And he was alive. With Joseph gone, he was the only boy in the family to carry on the Chartrand name. How could he not care about him? Family to him had always been the most important thing.

"Are you all right?" Her voice sounded gentle, concerned.

"No, I'm not all right. How can I be?"

She reached out and put her hand on his arm. He wanted to pull away but didn't. "I am sorry if I upset you, Mr. Chartrand. I realize your brother's murder is a great tragedy, but so is my sister's death. I loved her very much. She was my youngest sister."

"Your sister was murdered by overzealous misled religious fanatics because she loved a foreigner. What was the reason for my brother's murder?"

Kalila shrugged. "I do not know that. Not for certain, anyway."

"Then you know something?"

She nodded. "Your brother was involved in things he should not have been involved in."

"Like what?"

"We believe that he and a number of other American soldiers were selling weapons to insurgents."

"I don't believe that! Not my brother. He fought the insurgents. He would never sell weapons to his enemies to be used against him and his American fellow soldiers."

"Good people sometimes do unexplainable things for different reasons. Money, for instance. Or maybe he became disillusioned with this conflict between our countries?"

Jeff gave her a long hard look. "Who the hell are you really? You didn't come all the way from Iraq to tell me that my brother shacked up with your sister and had an illegal son with her?"

"You are correct, I did not, but everything I told you so far is true." She paused. "I am working for Iraqi Intelligence. My reason for coming to your country is to try to stop the trade of illegal arms. We are as concerned as you Americans are about supplying weapons to Iraqi insurgents. I want to find out who is behind it."

"And you think I'm involved?"

"Not you, however your brother was. We have proof. One of our undercover agents infiltrated a group of insurgents, who bought weapons from American soldiers." She smiled sadly. "I am sorry."

Jeff recalled the pictures on the SD card. Who took them? Michael? That meant he had been there. The evidence pointed in that direction, but Jeff still refused to believe in his brother's involvement.

Not Michael!

Then he remembered the bank account MacKay had shown him. With his and Michael's name on it. He remembered the large sum of money it contained. Had that account been opened by Michael?

"I still don't believe my brother was involved in the illegal arms trade," he said slowly. "There has to be another explanation."

She gave him a quick smile. "Well, maybe then you should try to find out what exactly it was your brother did in Iraq. And here at home."

"He was a mechanic, damn it. Also a family man. Ever since he came back home, he never left the country again. How could he have been selling weapons to anyone? He was too busy re-building that old Corvette of his."

Jeff was ready to smash his fist into the dashboard, or maybe slap this woman, who looked at him with her dark, haunting eyes, pitying him in his agony. He didn't want her pity. "I would have known something wasn't right. His wife would have known."

"Perhaps she did."

"No way! No fucking, fucking way!"

Her face showed disapproval and even shock by his sudden use of profane language. "Why do you Americans resort to using such language when you get angry?" she asked.

"Better than blowing up planes or beating your wife. Or stone to death a young woman who fell in love with the wrong guy, isn't it?" he countered angrily.

She didn't comment, just kept looking at him. He found her suddenly terribly attractive and desirable. "You look a lot like your sister," he said with a quiet voice, his anger draining away. "I can see why my brother fell in love with her. Those dark nights in the desert can get lonely."

Her smile was genuine. "You have been in the desert?"

"In Kuwait. Sixteen years ago. I'm surprised you didn't know that, since you seem to know everything else about me."

"I know very little about you besides the fact that you are Michael's brother and a policeman. I was not briefed about you because my presence here is not really official."

"What exactly is it you want from me?" he asked.

"From you? Right now, nothing. I just wanted to meet you." She smiled. "After all, we do have something in common...one little boy." She reached into her purse, took out a pen and a small notepad. After scribbling something on it, she handed him one of the notes. "I am staying at this hotel for a few days. Here is the number, in case you want to reach me."

"Why would I want to do that?"

She shrugged. "I do not know but in case you do."

He watched her walking across the parking lot toward her car. Rented of course. He wondered if she owned a car in Iraq, since woman in that country had been threatened with violence if they ever got behind the wheel of a car.

The rain had stopped completely and he decided to drive to his sister's place.

Chapter Fifteen

Helmut wasn't home. He and his old School-chum Herr Reinhart had gone out for a beer.

"I'm surprised," Jeff chuckled. "I thought Helmut didn't like our American beer?"

Barbara laughed. "He's been known to drink it in a pinch. Besides, Reinhart isn't that fussy. He drinks anything and more." She looked intently into his face. "You look troubled. Something wrong, Jeff?"

"There is some stuff I have to tell you," he said. "Apparently, our brother Michael was not the wonderful family man and devoted husband we thought he was."

"What are you trying to say?"

He pulled out the envelope Kalila gave him and deposited the pictures on the coffee table. "Take a look at those." Watching his sister's reaction with some trepidation, he expected her to be upset when he told her what the pictures represented.

Barbara went through the pictures, studying each one carefully. Looking up, she asked, "Who is that woman with Michael? She looks like one of those Muslim women."

"Her name is Adira Ahmed. She is an Iraqi and she was Michael's lover."

Barbara put her hand over her mouth. "His lover? How do you know?" She didn't seem as horrified of the news as he had expected.

"Michael had pictures of her among his stuff I picked up at the garage. When I saw them, I had my suspicions. They were confirmed today. I spoke with Adira's sister. By the way, Adira is dead. Murdered by her own people for sleeping with an American."

"How awful!"

122

"It's called honor-killing. Saddam Hussein made it legal in 1991. I read somewhere that over fifty women were publicly beheaded in Baghdad alone because they were suspected of immorality. Suspected!"

"Those Muslims are horrible people. How can they justify that? All in the name of their god. How can a true God let things like that happen? We should just nuke the whole damn place and be done with it." She sounded upset and her eyes blazed fiercely as she spoke.

"Be careful making such a statement, Barb. I can't believe every Muslim condones this barbaric practice." Jeff shook his head. "Unfortunately, because of Islamic extremists who treat women as second class citizens and who don't seem to value life the way we do, we condemn every Muslim. Remember the Romans, who threw Christians to the lions? That didn't make every Roman citizen an evil, bloodthirsty monster. Besides, our own Christian God doesn't exactly prevent horrible deeds from happening."

Barbara sighed. "You're right. I'm sure this young Iraqi woman was a good person." She stared at Jeff. "I'm so disappointed in Michael, though. I mean, being married to Samantha and all. How could he do that to her?"

"Being away from home and in a foreign land makes men…" he smiled, "…and sometimes women…do things that don't make much sense. Soldiers face death at every corner. They have few pleasant days and when a bit of sunshine comes their way they take and cherish it. It is not always the right thing."

"Why, what did you do when you where in Kuwait?"

"Nothing like that, but I know some of my buddies who did. Besides, I wasn't married then."

Barbara scrutinized the picture of the little boy with sudden interest. "I'm afraid to ask who this little boy is."

"His name is Omar. That's Michael's son."

"Oh, my god. Michael had a kid with her. A son. Is he alive?"

Jeff nodded. "He's in an orphanage in Afghanistan."

"In an orphanage? Oh, Jeff, Jeff. We have to bring him home." She burst into tears. "We can't let him grow up in an orphanage, raised in the Muslim faith. He might even become a member of those terrible Taliban some day. We can't let that happen. Not Michael's son. He is our blood. He needs to be with his family."

Barbara's reaction didn't surprise Jeff. He had pretty much expected it. She had a big heart with much love to give, and family to her was even more important than it was to him.

"I know, Sis, I've had the same thoughts, but we can't just fly there and get him."

"Why not?"

Jeff lifted his hands in resignation. "Because there are proper channels to follow. Adoption papers. Lawyers. Possibly bribing some people. We don't even know where exactly he is."

"Then we must find out. You spoke to his mother's sister. She'll probably know. We can't just shrug this off." Her tears were flowing freely as she looked at the picture of her dead brother's son. Her fingers stroked the image of the little boy with the large blue eyes…the eyes of her brother.

"I'm not shrugging it off. All I'm saying is don't get your hopes up." He debated if he should tell her the rest, but then he decided she had a right to know. Nothing was to be gained by keeping it a secret. "It seems Michael was involved in selling weapons to the Iraqi underground."

Barbara was even less ready to accept it than he had been, and the accusation visibly upset her. "That is something I don't believe. Michael would never betray his country. He loved it too much. He would never sell us out."

"That's what I said." He didn't tell her about the other things he'd seen on the SD card…the dead civilians, the rape and murder of the Iraqi girl, the pictures of a possible arms deal. No need to burden her with that.

Laughter from the basement told him that the girls were still up. "You can't possibly be thinking of adopting that little boy," he said. "Not with three children already."

"There is no one else, Jeff. You certainly can't do it." She chuckled, drying her tears with the sleeve of her blouse. "The girls are old enough. They can help me look after him." She became suddenly serious. "That man phoned again. Said his boss is getting impatient. He wants his money otherwise he may just have to resort to extreme measures."

"Extreme measures? Did he elaborate?"

"No. Isn't it enough that he phoned and threatened me again?"

124

"That son of a bitch!" Jeff pounded his fist into his palm. "I guess he needs to be taught another lesson…one he won't forget easily."

"Don't get yourself into more trouble than you are already in, Jeff. You're on suspension. Let the police handle it." She sounded concerned, and rightfully so. He had to tread carefully. Lieutenant Beacher had not been happy about his little excursion, and Captain Stoneman would only protect him as long as he didn't become a liability and possibly threaten the Captain's own career.

However, on the other hand, he could not ignore the threat. Galliano would never give up, already out of principal. If he let this one slip, his reputation would suffer. And Tony Moretti? He would be only too happy to oblige his boss and do something stupid. No, Jeff could not let it pass. He knew the police department wouldn't do anything about it. Galliano had connections. Jeff had found that out already.

Damn it! What a mess. He didn't need this right now. "I'd better go home," he told Barbara. "It's been a long day and I'm really tired." He kissed her on the cheek. "I'll take care of the problem. And don't worry. I'll be careful."

"Please, try to find out where our little boy is, Jeff. I won't be able to think straight until I know we can do something for him." Barbara wiped her eyes. She could get very emotional about things, and this was something she suddenly cared about. He knew she wouldn't rest until he satisfied her wish.

"I'll try, Sis. Just don't drive yourself crazy now, okay?"

He drove home, his radio turned up loud so he wouldn't have to think too much. When he arrived home, he searched in his pockets for the note Kalila gave him and put it on his dresser. He'd phone her hotel in the morning. Maybe she could help him.

Even though his thoughts were in turmoil, he slept soundly that night. Never woke up until five in the morning. Daylight peeked already in through the curtains, but he managed to sleep another couple of hours. Then he got up, took a shower and felt much better than the day before. He decided to go out for breakfast, since his fridge was nearly empty. Checking his watch, he noticed that it was close to eight. Not too early to make his call.

The desk clerk at the hotel put him through to Kalila's room. She answered it immediately, sounding wide-awake.

"Jeff Chartrand here. I hope I didn't wake you up."

She chuckled into the phone. "No, you did not. I am an early riser, even though I am still suffering a bit from jetlag. What can I do for you?"

"I'd like to know where my brother's son is right now," he said, coming right down to the reason of his call.

There was a pause at the other end. "His name is Omar," Kalila said softly. "Why not call him by his name?"

"Okay. Do you know where he is?"

"Yes, I do. Why?"

"My sister thinks he should not grow up in an orphanage. She wants to adopt him."

"Your sister is very kind. She will not regret her decision, I promise you." She paused again. "You know, I love him, too. After all, he is my nephew, also, not just yours. He is the only good thing I have left of my sister."

"I'll be going for breakfast. Would you like to join me? The place I go to is across the street from my building. Why don't you meet me there, say, in about an hour?"

"I will. Good bye till then."

She hung up and he listened to the phone for a moment, wondering if his line was still bugged. It didn't matter. His building was probably under surveillance anyway and his meeting with Kalila would not go unnoticed.

He waited for her outside the coffee shop. She was there at exactly one hour after she hung up the phone. Smiling at him, she gave him a little nod. "Good morning, Mr. Chartrand. Did you have a good night's rest?"

He held the door open for her and she walked into the room ahead of him. "Where do you want to sit?" she asked him.

He indicated a table in the far corner. "Over there will be fine."

She seemed to hesitate, but then she shrugged and walked toward the table. Sitting down, she said, "I am not used to the American customs. Does a woman sit down before the man does, or is it the opposite?"

He grinned. "There are no rules. A gentleman will let a woman sit down first. He will hold the chair for her until she is seated. Since there are only booths here, I can't do that for you. Ever since the Women's Rights Movement began, many things have changed. A man usually doesn't hold the door open anymore for a woman, or give her his seat on the bus. However, a gentleman and civilized man will still do those things." He smiled and shrugged. "Unless the woman objects to being treated like a lady. It happens. Some women are actually offended if a man holds open the door for her or offers her his seat. Go figure."

She smiled at him. "You Americans. Who can figure you out?" She gave him a curious look. "You act differently today. Your hostility toward me seems to have disappeared."

"A good night's rest will do that. In addition, I had time to figure out some things. I realized you are not my enemy. At least I hope not."

"I am not." Her smile lit up her face and her dark eyes seemed to mock him a little. "We are related now. How can we be enemies?" She became serious. "You told me on the phone your sister wants to adopt Omar. Is that her sincere wish?"

"Oh, believe me, it is. My sister is like a bulldog, once she has made up her mind that she wants something she'll go for it and she won't let go until she has it." His smile was not gentle as his thoughts wandered briefly to Galliano. *I suffer from the same affliction. I won't let go either.*

"I would like to meet your sister sometime. I am sure she is very beautiful, judging by your and your brother's handsome appearance."

Her comment surprised him a little. "For an Iraqi woman who's supposed to be oppressed, you are not shy giving a man compliments," he said.

"I am not your average Iraqi woman," she said. "My mother was a highly educated woman. She had a doctorate and used to wear short skirts in her younger days. That is all changed now."

"What does your father do?"

"He is a Judge."

"Not a very safe position these days in Iraq, is it?"

"No position is safe these days in Iraq, Mr. Chartrand."

"Call me Jeff. As you said, we are related." He gave her a friendly smile. "Can I call you Kalila or is that against some Islamic decree?"

"You may call me Kalila. I would prefer you do so, anyway."

Jeff looked up when the waitress came to take their order. "Do you drink coffee?" he asked Kalila.

"Not for breakfast. In my country, we drink coffee only once a day, in the afternoon when we have visitors. However, I would like a cup of tea and maybe a biscuit if you do not mind."

"Why should I? Do you mind if I order bacon and eggs?" he asked.

"It is your country, Jeff. Eat what you are accustomed to." She gave him a little smile. "I am not here to change your customs and your way of life. I am only a visitor."

He didn't comment, because he knew what she meant. Westerners seemed to make it a habit of sending people to other countries to impose their own way of life. Missionaries have been doing it for hundreds of years. Trying to change people who were perfectly happy with the way they lived. He looked at the waitress. "Bacon and eggs for me, easy over, and coffee, black. Tea and biscuits for the lady."

"Coming right up."

Kalila watched the girl walking away. "She is lucky," she said. "She can show off her nice legs, display her beautiful long hair and face without fearing to offend anyone."

"I thought women in those Middle East countries enjoyed covering up their bodies and faces," Jeff said.

"Some do, but many object to that rule. I do. My mother does. Even my father supports our views. He is quite liberated, but he cannot change anything, not by himself. Even he has to fear for his life if he speaks out against the clergy and the politicians." She sighed. "Iraq used to be one of the most progressive Middle Eastern countries. Now everything has changed. You told me that here in America the Women's Rights Movement changed things for the women…well, much has also changed in Iraq, but more radical and not for the better. Here women gained more freedom, in my country women are afraid to go out for fear of being raped or kidnapped."

"That is why our troops are in your country. To bring order and to set your people free." When he said that he felt like someone trying to justify America's presence in Iraq. It suddenly sounded phony in his ears. He gave her a crooked grin.

She shook her head. "Many of my people feel it would have been better if the Americans had left Saddam Hussein alone. He was an evil man, but at least he kept order in the country. Right now, we live in an almost lawless society, with sectarian warfare escalating. We do not know where and how it will end."

"You know, there are many Americans who will tell you the same thing. Many are against the war in Iraq and many warned our government that it would not end well. They predicted another Vietnam."

"What do you believe, Jeff?"

He shrugged. "I fought in Kuwait. I thought I did the right thing. My brother fought in Iraq. He believed he did the right thing. I lost friends in that war. Am I going to tell their wives and families it was all for nothing? That their husbands, fathers, brothers, and friends gave their life for a mistake our politicians made?" He shook his head. "I can't tell you what I really think, because I don't know myself."

The waitress brought their food and Jeff was grateful for the interruption. He dug into his bacon and eggs with gusto. Somehow, the presence of Kalila didn't seem to bother him this morning. Maybe he was getting used to her already. He studied her features as she daintily ate her biscuits and sipped her tea.

She had a straight nose and beautiful eyes, full lips. Her smile enchanted him and he had to keep himself from staring too long. She could have won any beauty contest she entered. Her body wasn't hard to look at either. Even though she wore a loose blouse, it was evident by the way they stood away from her chest that she had a nice pair of breasts. She wore slacks, but he would have bet that she had great legs.

"Is something wrong?" she asked.

"No, why?"

"Because you have been staring at me."

"Oh," he laughed, embarrassed. "I was just wondering about something. Where did your sister meet Michael?"

"Adira was an interpreter working for the Americans."

"I see. She must have been very smart. It is not easy to translate languages fluently. I've always admired people who could do that."

"She was smart. And she loved life. Maybe a little too much." Her dark eyes became even darker. "I am not blaming your brother for having an affair with my sister. Had it not been him, she might have picked someone else. She was a little…wild."

"And you?" He looked at her.

"What about me?"

He almost asked her if she also was wild but changed his mind. "Are you married?"

"No. There is no room in my life for a man. Not with my job."

"Oh, right. You are an undercover agent. I almost forgot." He gave her a thoughtful look. "How did you get into our country? It must be awfully hard for an Iraqi to come here. Let's face it…Iraqis do not usually visit our country, not anymore. And a woman all by herself? How did you manage that?"

She smiled. "I had help. I actually do possess an American passport. A forgery but a very good one, obviously."

"Obviously. Aren't you taking a chance telling me this? After all, I am a cop. I could arrest you right now."

"I trust you that you will not. Besides, you have been suspended."

"You know about that? I thought you didn't know anything about me?"

"I lied a little." She shrugged. "I know that you are being watched by your government right now. They suspect you of having dealings with terrorists because of your brother."

"And you believe that also?"

"No. I do not. Unless my information about you is wrong."

"Where did you get your information?"

"I cannot tell you that. But I have a feeling we will be seeing more of each other." Her smile looked mysterious. Then she laughed. "You should see your face now. Like someone who has been told a bad joke. Am I such bad company?"

"No, in fact, you are pleasant enough, but you have a strange way of talking and I don't mean your accent. Under different circumstances, I would try to get you into my bed, but since I know where you come from, I'm not going to waste energy and effort. You are a beautiful and mysterious woman."

"And you are quite forward, Mr. Chartrand." She didn't seem offended by what he'd told her.

"I thought we were on first name basis, Kalila, or should I call you Miss Ahmed again?"

Her eyes looked into his. "You can still call me Kalila, Jeff."

She rose. "I must go now. I have an appointment today, which I do not want to miss." She held out a hand. "Good bye, Jeff. And thank you for breakfast."

"You never told me where I can find Omar?"

"No, I have not. I will tell you, but at another time. We have much to discuss. I will contact you."

She turned and walked away. He watched her, shaking his head. He meant it when he told her about trying to get her into his bed. She seemed to be a woman full of deep passion and capable of satisfying a man.

Too bad, she isn't an American. Or at least any other nationality, except Iraqi.

He ordered another cup of coffee and sat thinking about the last few days. The days ahead didn't look too bright.

He paid and left the coffee shop. He started to cross the street, when someone said beside him, "May we have a word with you, Mr. Chartrand?"

He turned to look at the speaker, a tall bearded gentleman, dressed in a dark suit, wearing dark glasses. At first, Jeff thought he was a government agent, but then he realized his mistake. The man had spoken with an Eastern accent, the same accent as that spoken by Kalila. The man also sprouted a beard and wore a dark suit.

"Depends," Jeff said. He moved back onto the sidewalk, watching both men warily, his body relaxed but ready to explode into action if necessary.

The first man noticed Jeff's stance and stepped back, holding up a hand. "We are not here to start a fight with you. We just want to talk."

"About what?" Jeff wasn't taken in that easily.

"An arrangement. A business deal." The man indicated the door into the coffee shop. "Shall we go inside? We can talk in there."

"What if I refuse?"

The man chuckled. "Then you will have to deal with the consequences. They will not be pleasant, I can promise you that. Consequences for you and others. I think you understand."

"A threat?"

"No. A warning." His hand pointed at the door. "Do it the easy way and we will all be happy."

Jeff shrugged. What the hell! He took offence to being threatened. However, an unknown threat is impossible to deal with. He needed to know more about these two men and what they wanted from him.

As it happened, the same table he vacated only minutes before was still available. The waitress was just wiping the top when she saw him approach. Smiling at him, she said, "You're back. Is everything all right?"

"Everything is fine," he told her. "I just ran into some old friends. Bring me another coffee and tea for the gentlemen." He slid into the seat and looked at the two men expectantly. "Well, sit down. I might even pay for your tea if what you tell me meets with my approval."

"We will not take long," the first man said.

Both men took a seat across from him.

"What can I do for you gentlemen?" Jeff asked, rubbing his hands, acting jovially. "I have a feeling in my guts that it won't be anything good, but I'm willing to listen."

"Mr. Chartrand, are you an honorable man?" the first man asked.

Jeff wondered if the other one ever spoke. "I think so," he told them, looking from one to the other.

"If that is true we will not have a problem."

"Perhaps if you'd tell me what you are talking about, maybe then we can clear up this mystery."

The man smiled. "There is no mystery here. We deposited twenty thousand dollars into your brother's bank account. We did not receive anything for it."

A cold shiver ran down Jeff's spine. He would finally find out about the money and he knew he would not be happy about it. "Why would you deposit that kind of money into my brother's account?" he asked.

"We had a contract with him."

"I know nothing about a contract. Sorry, I guess you're outa luck there."

"Do not play stupid, Mr. Chartrand. We understand you are the executer of your late brother's estate. Are we correct?"

"You are, but that still doesn't mean I know about everything my brother was involved in. Why don't you enlighten me?"

"All right, we will play your little game." The man leaned forward, smiled, like a long lost friend. "We represent a group of people who are involved in a conflict with a hostile invader of our country. To fight this war we need weapons, lots of them. We also need ammunition. Your brother was, how shall we say, he was the liaison officer between us and the company we are doing business with here in America. He arranged the financial transactions. The twenty thousand dollars we recently deposited in his account is his broker's fee. As I have said, we did not get anything in return. Now we want our money back."

"I don't know what you are talking about, Mister…? You never told me your name."

"My name is unimportant."

"Well, then, Mister with no name, my brother never told me about this thing. I don't have the faintest idea about any of this. You'll have to give me a few more details about yourself and why you've paid my brother. Once I'm satisfied that the money is really yours and if you give me an account number, you will receive your money back."

The man leaned back into his seat and let out a short burst of laughter. "Do not try to play games with us, Mr. Chartrand!" he said with a snarl. "You know, I am losing my patience, and I am a very patient man. I suggest you begin making arrangements." He looked at his silent companion. "Let us go."

Both men rose. The first man threw a card on the table. "That is the account number with a bank in the Cayman Islands. We expect action within a couple of weeks. You will not be contacted again by us, not directly, but if you fail to deliver, you will suffer the consequences. Am I making myself clear?"

"Crystal. But let me tell you something. Now that you've made me aware of your existence, I will watch out for you. I am not an easy target. If anything should happen to any of my friends or relatives, I will come hunting for you and your people, wherever they and you are. I will find you. Is that clear?"

The man pulled his lips into a sneer. "You are not in a very good position to threaten us, Mr. Chartrand. So be a good boy and do as we ask. Have a nice day." He gave him a mock salute and walked away from the table, followed by his companion.

When the waitress came with his coffee and the two cups of tea, she looked puzzled at the two empty seats. "They were in a hurry," Jeff said, "but don't worry, I'll pay for their tea."

He sat silently drinking his coffee. Fuck it! Things were getting more and more complicated. It didn't take a genius to figure out whom those two goons represented.

Iraqi insurgents? Al Qaeda? Taliban? Hamas? It didn't matter. They were all considered terrorists and bad news. This confirmed that Michael had been involved in an ugly affair. Who would have thought? And yet, something about this whole business bothered Jeff. He was still not willing to believe that his brother would do such a thing. And if he did, he must have had a good reason.

He finished his coffee and left the coffee shop again. This time he looked around before crossing the street, almost expecting to have someone else accost him, but nobody did. Remembering his promise to Barbara, he picked up his key and went down into the basement area where he rented a small storage area. It wasn't much larger than a tiny closet but big enough to hold some of the stuff he seldom needed. He found the small box he was looking for and took out the Smith & Wesson he kept hidden in there, shoved it into his belt and went into the parking garage to get his car.

He had no intentions of shooting anyone, but he wasn't going into the lion's den without adequate backup.

It had begun raining again. This was not a good day; even the weather didn't cooperate. He didn't phone anyone this time to announce his impending visit.

The parking lot of the Three Palms Casino was already filled almost to capacity with cars. Gambling was good business. People liked to lose their money. Everybody dreamed about winning the jackpot. Few ever did.

Out of habit, he took the safety off his gun before he walked into the building. Surprisingly, nobody guarded the door into Galliano's private office, and Jeff walked right in. Galliano wasn't alone. The woman was there again, but this time she was completely naked. She sat on the edge of the desk, Galliano stood between her spread thighs, his pants around his ankles and his big fat white buttocks moving slowly back and forth.

They never knew Jeff was there until he stepped to the other side of the desk and said, "I'd like to have a word, Mr. Galliano, or is this a bad time?"

The fat man froze. "What the hell!"

"Don't stop on account of me, Mr. Galliano. I can wait until you finish up." Jeff lowered himself into Galliano's big chair. "This is a nice and comfortable chair," he commented. "You're a lucky man in many ways. I mean…a fat guy like you getting the opportunity to fuck a beautiful woman like that? Yeah, you're lucky. Not everybody is this lucky."

The woman on the desk sat rigid. She stared at Jeff for a moment, then she relaxed and burst out laughing. "My horoscope told me I would meet a tall dark stranger today. I guess that would be you, although you've been here before. I imagined it to happen under different circumstances."

Galliano was still standing between the woman's open legs. "Are you some kind of fucking voyeur? Get the fuck out of my chair and my office!"

"I will. After I've had my talk with you."

"I'm standing here with my pants down, you fucking moron," Galliano said indignantly.

"I'm not stopping you from pulling them up." Jeff gave a little chuckle. "Should I get a pail of water?"

"Oh, shut up!" Galliano moved away from the woman and pulled up his pants.

"What about me?" the woman asked. "Should I wait until you guys are finished talking?"

Galliano stared at her. "Are you fucking nuts? Get dressed and get the hell out!"

"She can stay as far as I'm concerned," Jeff said, smirking.

The woman smiled at him. Then she slid off the desk and, with swinging hips, she walked over to a chair, picked up her dress and slipped into it. "Nice meeting you," she said to Jeff. "Perhaps we'll run into each other again. Perhaps next time you and I…"

"Get out, you dumb broad!" Galliano snarled. He stared at Jeff. "And you…get out of my chair!"

"I'm comfortable," Jeff said, but then he got up and walked around the desk to take another chair. He watched Galliano sprawl into his own chair.

"What do you want?" the fat man wheezed.

Jeff sat relaxed but kept a wary eye on the man. "I guess you remember my name?" he asked.

"How the fuck can I forget. Your brother owes me a lot of money, Chartrand."

"Five thousand bucks, plus a reasonable amount of interest. Legally, you don't have a leg to stand on, but I'm willing to pay the money when the government releases my brother's estate. I told you that the last time I was here." He paused. "However, you refuse to understand the problem. You are harassing my sister, have threatened her and her family."

"I haven't threatened anyone. I just want my money."

"And you'll get it."

"So what's the problem, Chartrand?"

"Time. Only time."

Galliano leaned forward. His little pig's eyes seemed even smaller. "Take all the time you want, but remember, the more time you take, the more you owe me. I'm a businessman, not a banker. May I suggest you take a loan until your brother's money is released?"

Jeff allowed himself a small chuckle. This man was beginning to irritate him. "When pigs fly, Mr. Galliano. Perhaps you should grow some wings. It would make a good start."

"What?"

A noise from the door made Jeff turn. When he saw Tony Moretti, Galliano's guard, walking in, he instinctively reached for his gun but didn't draw it from his belt. Tony looked at Jeff in surprise. "What the fuck?"

"Shoot the son of a bitch!" Galliano screamed.

Out of the corner of his eye, Jeff saw Galliano bring up his hand from under his desk. He saw the object in the fat man's hand, reacted instinctively. Pulling his gun, he brought it up, fired without thinking. Then he swung it around, registered the gun in Tony's hand, fired again, watched the big man fall.

Everything seemed to happen in slow motion, but it was over before he realized what took place. Galliano lay slumped over his desk. Jeff knew the fat man was dead even before he saw the dark pool on the desktop. A bullet into the brain will do that.

He got up, walked over to Tony. He had acted automatically; there had been no time to think where he should aim. His training had taken over. He had shot to kill, not to maim. The way Tony lay on the floor, he had no doubts that he was dead, too.

A dark stain seeping from Tony's chest painted the light carpet red. When Jeff turned the man over, he looked into his slack face. The eyes were open, unseeing.

He didn't bother to check Galliano.

Fuck it! This had not been his intention. He came here to talk, not to kill. Sitting down in a chair, he pulled out his cell phone and dialed his precinct. "I want to report a shooting."

Chapter Sixteen

He hadn't moved from his chair when the door opened and two cops walked in. Maxine was one of them. She and her partner had their guns out, aimed at Jeff.

"My gun is over there on the desk. I'm unarmed," Jeff told them.

Maxine walked up to him, her face an unreadable mask. "Stand up, please."

He looked at her. "It's me, Max. There is no need for this."

"You have the right to remain silent…"

"I know the routine. Are you arresting me?"

"Please refer to me as Detective Montana. Anything you say can be used against you…"

"Aren't you even going to listen to what happened here?" He didn't believe what was happening could be real. This was the woman he had slept with, been intimate with. She couldn't possibly be as cold as she pretended.

"Two men are dead. You shot them. That's what happened here. You can tell your side of the story to the investigating officer," she said with the voice of a stranger.

"Not you?"

"No. Now, please turn around." Her voice didn't betray any emotion.

Jeff was ready to burst out laughing when she put the cuffs on him and read him his rights. He felt like being in a nightmare or in some kind of B-grade crime drama. This was definitely not a good day. He didn't know the cop with Maxine. "My ex-partner doesn't seem to recognize me," Jeff said. "And you probably never heard of me, but I'm a cop, like you. So give me some slack. Don't treat me like a common criminal."

The detective looked at him, shaking his head. "I've heard about you, Chartrand. Don't expect any special treatment. You'll be treated like any other suspect." He turned and addressed two other cops who came walking into the room. "Take him away. And watch him. He's dangerous."

Jeff gave him a sharp look. "Thanks, buddy. I'll remember this. I have a good memory for faces. Maybe some day I can repay the favor." His gaze lingered on Maxine. She returned his look, her face a mask, her eyes cool. He wanted to say something but refrained.

Shrugging, he let the two young cops push him through the door. The gaming room was strangely silent. Everyone watched him being led out of the casino. He was surprised to see a news-van outside with reporters and cameramen.

Somebody had leaked information. He smiled grimly. His face would be plastered all over the six o'clock news. This definitely did not look good. Galliano had many friends, the Mayor and the DA among them. His death was going to create unpleasant ripples. Galliano would be painted as a saint. And Jeff? Well…he didn't need much of an imagination. His ass was in a sling. Even a miracle may not be able to save him now.

Holding a hand over his face, he climbed into the back seat of the police cruiser. They took him to a different precinct, where they took his mug shot and fingerprinted him.

"Empty your pockets, take off your belt, and hand over your wallet," the booking sergeant told him.

Jeff did as asked, watching the officer put it all into a plastic bag.

"And your watch."

"I prefer to hang on to it." Jeff had his reasons. That watch was more than just a timepiece. He didn't need anyone to give it a closer examination. By now, his arrest had been recorded and, hopefully, alerted somebody to his predicament and whereabouts. It also pretty much determined which steps he needed to take in the near future.

The officer stared at him, a smirk on his face. "We have rules here, buddy. Let's have the watch."

Reluctantly, Jeff gave it to him. Best not to make a big fuss, or someone might just wonder what made his watch so important.

They put him into a holding cell. Before the guard closed the door, Jeff asked for a lawyer.

"What's your hurry? You're not going anywhere. You'll get one in due time."

"How about my call?"

"In due time. We're awfully busy right now." The guard grinned. "You're a cop. You know how it is."

The door shut with a dull clank, and the soft click of the lock made Jeff angry. They treated him like a drug-dealer, or worse, a crooked cop. Slamming his flat hand against the bars, he yelled, "Someone is going to pay for this!"

"Save your breath, buddy," said a voice behind him. "These guys won't give you a break."

Jeff turned around to look at the speaker. "Yeah, well, I tried. How about you? Did you get your one and only call?"

The man heaved his big bulk off the bench. Shrugging, he joined Jeff by the bars. "Ain't got nobody to call. No friends, no lawyer. I guess they'll supply me with a public defender."

"What did they nab you for?" Jeff asked.

The man grinned. "They say I relieved some old lady of her handbag."

"Did you?"

"Certainly not. It's all a big misunderstanding. You see, I found it on the bench in the park and I assumed somebody forgot it. So I opened it to see if I could find the rightful owner and return it. That's when this old hag comes screaming, pointing a finger at me, yelling I stole it. The cop who was with her didn't even give me a chance to explain. Just hauled my ass in here."

Jeff had to suppress a grin. The way the guy told it and his facial expression was just priceless. "I suppose you're innocent?"

"Of course I am." He put his hand over his heart. "I didn't even have time to count the money in her purse. Could have used some of that, you know, with me being down on my luck lately." He shuffled back to the bench and sat down.

Jeff didn't have to guess what this man did for a living. His clothing had seen better days and his face could use a razor to shave off the scraggly beard. And it would be best to stand up-wind from him.

He studied Jeff out of red-rimmed eyes. "I guess you wouldn't have a couple of bucks to spare, buddy? You look like you're doing well."

"They took all my stuff, including my wallet, at the desk," Jeff said, smiling.

"Too bad. Hey, maybe when you get out, leave a few bucks for me at the desk. Just to tie me over when they let me outta here. How about it?"

"Maybe I'll do just that," Jeff said. The man was a con artist, but he was harmless. Probably spend any money Jeff left him on booze the moment he got out.

"Do you mind if I stretch out here on this bench and get some rest? Haven't had a decent place to sleep for days now."

Jeff lifted his hand. "You just go ahead and take that nap. I don't mind."

It didn't take long until the man started snoring. Jeff folded his legs under him and sat cross-legged on the hard floor.

Damn! What a mess he had fallen into this time. He cursed Michael and that fat pig Galliano for being responsible. Galliano was a criminal and so was Tony Moretti. They got what they deserved, but the law would not see it that way. He had gone there as a private citizen, carrying a gun. A gun that wasn't even registered. Any prosecutor would use this as reason to have him put away for a long time.

If he got lucky, they might even charge him with Murder in the First Degree. By all appearances, he had gone there with the intent to kill.

Shit!

He figured about an hour went by when he heard the footsteps of someone coming down the corridor. It surprised him to see Maxine. She didn't smile.

The guard with her unlocked the cell door and told him to get out. Grinning, he said, "No funny stuff, okay?" The way he said it made Jeff wonder if he was hoping for a reason to use the flashlight he swirled in one hand.

"Don't worry. I'm not in a funny mood today," Jeff told him between clenched teeth and wondered if his remark could be used as an excuse. He was almost waiting for the guard to make his move. He needed a venue to vent his rage. Things couldn't possibly get any worse.

They took him into an interrogation room. Maxine sat at the table opposite from him. One wall was a mirror. Jeff tried to speculate who might be watching him from the other side.

"Nice to see you again, Miss Montana," Jeff said. "Did you come to apologize?"

"This is not a social call, and I have nothing to apologize for. I just did my job. You shot two people and I arrested you. You would have done the same thing had it been different."

"Meaning had you been the one doing the shooting?" He gave her a scrutinizing look. "I would not have let anyone intimidate me, Maxine," he said with a low voice.

"No one intimidated me."

"Right!" He looked at the mirror. "Who's on the other side? MacKay? Somebody from Internal Affairs?"

"There is nobody on the other side," she said, staring at him.

"Are you wearing a wire?" he asked.

She kept staring at him. Then he saw her almost indiscernible nod. Shrugging, he said, "It wouldn't really matter, because I have nothing of importance to tell you anyway. I have one request though. Can you have me transferred to another cell? My roommate snores and he smells like a cross between a brewery and a sewage treatment plant."

She actually allowed herself a tiny smile. "I'll see what I can do." Then, "Why did you do it?"

"Do what?"

"Shoot Galliano."

"For Christ sake, Maxine, it was an accident!" He had to keep himself from shouting. "I never went there to shoot anyone. They drew their guns first. I just reacted in defense."

"Why did you take a gun in the first place?"

His laughter sounded like the sound of a croaking frog in a deep well. "Would you jump into a pit filled with vipers without protection? Come on, Maxine. You know better than that. They taught us at that at the Academy. Always be prepared for the worst. I'd be dead now had I not carried my gun."

"An unregistered gun. You were warned to stay away from Galliano."

"He threatened my family."

"You should have let us handle it."

He laughed again. "How would you have handled it? Sent Galliano a letter of complaint? Dear Mr. Galliano, please stop making those annoying phone calls. Let's face it there was nothing anyone could have done, not legally."

She sighed. "You're in deep shit, Jeff."

The sudden use of his first name surprised him but also put him on the alert. She tried to put him into a relaxed mode, make him loose his caution. He might just give away personal information the people listening on the other side of the wire could use to their advantage.

She bent forward and spoke in a confidential tone. "How's your investigation into your brother's death going? Did you find any interesting stuff in his journal? What about the key?"

"The key?" Jeff hesitated. He had already told her about the key and about the SD card he found, and yet, she pretended not to know, possible proof that she had not sold him out, but also proof that she was not a free agent. She was being watched. "Oh, yes, the key. Sorry, I haven't had the chance to pursue that. I have no idea what it's for." He looked into her eyes and, his face away from the mirror, he mouthed, "I love you."

Her facial expression didn't change when she said, "I hope you're not chasing something unattainable. Things don't look promising." He thought he saw her eyes go moist and knew she wasn't talking about his investigation.

She blinked a few times, and then she rose. He felt like taking her into his arms, cover her face with kisses, taste her full lips and tell her everything was going to be all right. Instead, he sat rigid, agony filling his mind and making his body ache.

Oh, Max. I'm sorry I have dragged you into this. I love you so much, but I've treated you wrongly. You stayed loyal while I broke your trust in me. "I'm sorry," he said softly.

"For what?" She lifted an eyebrow.

"For everything. For the way things turned out. I should have listened to you when you told me not to go around beating up people." He smirked. "But I'm not a good listener."

Her back was to the mirror when she said, "You've always been stubborn." Before she turned away, her lips molded the words Love you. Then she rapped her knuckles against the door.

He studied her from the back as she waited. She carried her black coat over her arm, and he admired her round buttocks showing prominently even in her business suit. When she walked out of the door, he suffered a feeling of great loss. Would he ever be able to hold her in his arms again? Lose himself in her passionate embrace? Dig his fingers into those soft buttocks as she moved against him?

He barely paid attention when two armed guards walked in and escorted him back to his cell. His cellmate was gone and he didn't regret that at all. He needed to be alone, put things into perspective.

He slept on the vacated bench. It smelled of perspiration and stale alcohol. When he woke in the morning, his back felt as if someone had beaten him with a baseball bat all night long. An armed guard accompanied him to a bathroom. He felt better after he washed himself and combed his hair. There was nothing he could do about the stubble on his face. After breakfast, they came and took him back into the interrogation room.

He didn't have to wait long. When the door opened, a big, fat man stepped through. "I'm Elias Morgan. Your attorney," he introduced himself and took a seat opposite from Jeff.

"I guess I don't have to tell you who I am," Jeff said in a voice that indicated he didn't really care who the man was. If they thought they could get away with assigning some public advocate to represent him they were wrong.

"No, you don't, Mr. Chartrand. I know everything about you." The man seemed jovial. His round face beamed at Jeff. He came across like everybody's favorite uncle, but when Jeff looked into his gray eyes, he saw nothing but hardness.

"Who are you actually, Mr. Morgan?" Jeff asked. "Are you my public defender?"

Morgan smiled sparingly. "Hardly. I work for the law firm Cohen, Markus and Drexler."

"Never heard of them."

"I'd be surprised if you had. Our head office is located in Los Angeles."

"How did you get here so fast?"

"I have a small office in Sacramento." Morgan chuckled. "I don't like large offices."

"I didn't hire you." Jeff leaned back and gave the man a long stare. "What's your interest in me?"

Morgan opened his briefcase and pulled out a newspaper. Shoving it across the table, he said, "Have a look at this. You made front page."

Jeff stared at the paper, at the headline.

Ex-cop and recipient of Purple Heart arrested for the double murder of prominent businessman Joseph Galliano and his assistant Tony Moretti.

And then there was a large picture of him being escorted toward a waiting police cruiser.

...Jeff Chartrand, who was suspended for the shooting of ex-marine Ethan Grey two weeks ago, is suspected to have ties to the terrorist group known as Al Queda. Department of Homeland Security has not released any details, but Chartrand has been under investigation by both the FBI and Homeland Security...

He didn't bother reading the rest. He lifted his head to look at Morgan, who was watching him intently. "Where the hell did the press get a hold of this?"

Morgan shrugged. "Obviously, someone is feeding the press information. Right or wrong, it makes no difference. The press eats up stuff like this. It sells papers. It is also obvious someone wants your head. You've stepped into a cesspool of quicksand, my friend, and you need a life raft to save you. I'm that life raft."

"I don't know anything about you, Mr. Morgan. How do I know you have my best interest at heart?"

"You don't."

"Why do you want to represent me? What do you get out of it?"

"Yours is a high profile case, and defending you will give us international exposure. It will make us famous." Morgan's smile conveyed honesty and even some eagerness.

Jeff heard the words but didn't believe them. He didn't trust this man. "I'd like to think about it," he said.

Morgan shook his head. "Don't think too long. You'd be making a huge mistake not accepting our offer." He rose. "Good luck with whatever you decide, Mr. Chartrand. Oh..." He reached into the pocket of his fancy jacket. "Here is my business card."

* * * *

A new companion joined him in his cell in the afternoon. It took three officers to drag the man down the corridor. He was either drunk or high on something. Or maybe he was just a violent guy.

One of the guards unlocked his cuffs, and then they pushed him through the door. He stumbled, sprawled onto the hard floor, where he lay, cursing. "You motherfuckers, I'll sue you all," he shouted after them. Then he looked up and saw Jeff sitting on the bench. When Jeff smiled at him, he pointed a finger. "What are you grinning at?"

Jeff shrugged. "You and your antics. Save your breath and energy. Nobody gives a fuck."

The man sprang to his feet. Jeff was surprised at the agility he displayed. Crossing the distance between them in three steps, he stared down at Jeff, his eyes all crazy. Then he suddenly broke into an almost hysterical fit of laughter. Wiping his arm across his eyes, he said, "You're right, nobody does." He pointed his thumb across his shoulder. "Those cops are nothing but a bunch of morons."

He held out a hand. Jeff noticed the smoothness of the hand. Not the hand of a man who performs physical labor. "I'm Ronald Wilson. My friends call me Ronny."

Jeff shook the offered hand, noted the firm grip. "Jeff. Jeff Chartrand," he said.

"The name sounds familiar." He peered at Jeff. "I've seen you somewhere."

Jeff grinned. "Probably on TV. I'm famous, you know. My face was plastered all over the news this morning."

"The news?" Wilson's smooth face suddenly lit up. "Right, I remember now. You're the guy who wasted Galliano." His lips turned up into a part smile. "I knew the man. Rumor has it he had mob-connections. Are you by any chance a contract-man?"

"Are you suggesting somebody hired me to kill Galliano?" Jeff countered.

"I'm suggesting nothing, friend. Whatever reasons you had, I'm sure they were legit. Between you and me, the bastard probably deserved it." He paused, as a sudden thought seemed to pop into his mind. "They say you're an ex-cop."

"That's right. You don't like cops?" Jeff eyed him speculatively.

"Not particularly." Wilson chuckled. "Let's just say, me and the cops have different agendas."

"What do you do for a living?" Jeff asked, studying the man's impeccable clothes.

"I'm a professional gambler. A businessman."

"A con-man!" Jeff didn't hide his disapproval.

"That's a matter of opinion. I'm taking advantage of a situation when it is presented," Wilson defended himself. "Some people seem to take offense to that."

"So what got you arrested?"

"Some asshole suggested I cheated. You shouldn't play poker if you are not prepared to lose your money." Wilson shrugged. "Mind if I join you on that bench?"

Jeff moved over and made room for him to sit down. "I'm not a gambler," he said. "I don't even know how to play poker."

"No kidding? Everybody plays poker."

"I guess not everybody," Jeff said, laughing. "I've never cared much for playing any card games."

"What do you do in your spare time?"

"Shoot crooks." Jeff grinned. "Among other things."

"Like what?"

"I box. Practice martial arts, target shooting. That kind of stuff."

"That doesn't sound like much fun to me. Wouldn't that be considered just part of your job?" Wilson shook his head. "Not my kind of entertainment. Hey, maybe after we both get out, you and I can get together. Somebody needs to teach you some fun-stuff. You lead a boring life, my friend."

"Right now I have all the excitement I need, believe me." Jeff rose from the bench and stretched. "Besides, the way things stand right now, I may never see daylight again."

"According to the papers, you are a terrorist." Wilson looked up at Jeff, his eyes studying him with curiosity. "Any truth to that? I'm curious. Why would any red-blooded American even think about joining a terrorist group? I'm assuming you are an American."

Jeff snorted in disgust. "Of course I'm an American. Someone is spreading lies about me. Did you read the rest of the article?"

"As it happens, I did. Stuff like that has always interested me." He chuckled. "I may be considered a con-man, but I am a patriot. I love my country. Where else can an enterprising individual practice his craft unhindered? Only in the good ol' USA, the land of unlimited opportunities."

"Well, if you read the whole article, you'll know about my brother and his family."

Wilson nodded. "They say he also had ties to a foreign organization, before he and his family got wiped out."

"Murdered," Jeff said softly. "And there is no proof he ever was a traitor, like that article says." He pointed at the newspaper on the floor beside the bench. "Don't believe everything you read."

Wilson put up his hands. "I never said I believed it but others might. I don't envy you, my friend. My problems are nothing compared with yours. I only have one asshole to deal with. But you? Whoa! America is watching you."

"Yeah. Well. America may be doing better watching the real terrorists. My brother and I, we put in our time defending this country against terrorism, and this is how we get repaid," Jeff said bitterly.

"You and your brother must have done something to earn this kind of treatment," Wilson said. "Homeland Security would surely not put you on the watch list without good reason."

"For a guy who is busy relieving other people of their money, you seem to be quite informed about me and my predicament." Jeff gave the man an inquiring look, suspicion rising up inside him.

"I told you, I eat this kind of stuff. It interests me."

"Why?"

Wilson shrugged. "Information equals power. You never know when an opportunity arises. I like to be prepared for it." He peered up at Jeff. "Do you belief in luck?"

"Some people seem to be luckier than others."

"I don't believe in luck. I make it happen by being prepared. Sometimes the cards don't stack in your favor, but when you play them right, you can still come out a winner." Wilson shifted in his seat. "If you rely on luck alone you are betting on the wrong horse. The odds are not in your favor."

"Well, as I said, I'm not a gambler. I've never been to the horse races either."

"You are a dull person, my man." He leaned forward, and then he got off the bench. Standing in front of Jeff, he said, "I do not limit myself to just gambling. Sometimes I do small contract jobs. My present job seemed difficult at first. I waited for the right opportunity, took a bit of a gamble by possibly waiting too long, but it paid off. Suddenly, a window opened unexpectedly and made my job a hell of lot easier than anticipated. Almost too easy. In a way I feel a bit letdown because I do like a challenge. It's more fun."

"I don't have the faintest clue what you're talking about." Jeff took a small step backward. He never liked it when someone crowded him, but that was not the only reason. Wilson's demeanor had changed. Gone was that let's-be-friends-look. His face had lost all expression and his eyes seemed as frigid as a glacier.

"Would you like to know what my job is?" Wilson asked.

"Not particularly, but tell me if you must."

"It's nothing personal. I actually was beginning to like you. Under different circumstances, we might even become friends, and it seems you do need friends badly. You're not very popular with some people, you know."

Jeff saw something gleaming in Wilson's hand and acted instinctively. Grabbing the man's wrist with his left, he twisted, pulled the arm behind Wilson's back. His right arm shot up, and, pressing his forearm into the man's throat, he pushed him against the wall.

Wilson brought up his knee to smash it into Jeff's genitals, but he had anticipated it and blocked the man's knee with his own. Increasing his pressure on Wilson's throat, he snarled, "Who sent you?"

Wilson struggled, but Jeff was furious, pissed off at himself for almost being taken off guard by someone who had pretended to be just a friendly and sympathetic cellmate. "Who the fuck sent you? I am losing my patience. Talk or I'll crush your windpipe, you son of a bitch!"

The other man emitted choking sounds and clawed at Jeff's arm with his free hand. Jeff pulled on Wilson's arm, which he had pinned behind the man's back, and brought it to the front. Looking at the long needle, he said, "I guess that was supposed to be for my neck. Looks like your luck ran out today. Didn't play your cards right this time. You should have used it the moment you entered my cell, when I was still unaware of your intentions. You just seemed to show too much interest in me. I may not be a poker player, but I can read people."

Wilson had relaxed his leg and his crotch was unprotected. Jeff brought up his knee and put his full weight behind it. Wilson gave a choking cry and collapsed. Jeff let him slide to the ground, gave him another kick between the ribs with his foot, releasing his anger at Wilson and the rest of the world.

Breathing hard, he stepped back, the long needle in his hand. It had a rubber grip on one end. He must have hidden it inside the sleeve of his jacket.

He was right, those cops are a bunch of morons, Jeff thought, but he couldn't really blame them. How often do they have to deal with an assassin?

He studied the man on the ground. He was out cold, his face slack. A little blue from lack of oxygen, but he'd be all right. His balls would be sore for a long time. I hope I compressed them into tiny marbles, you son of a bitch. The anger boiled over in him and he felt like grabbing the man and smashing his head against the concrete floor until it burst like a ripe melon.

Sitting down on the bench, he knew he needed to get out of here. Getting up, he pulled Wilson to the bench and laid him on it. Then he went to the cell door and kicked it with his foot, making it rattle. "I want to call my lawyer," he yelled.

It didn't take long until one of the guards came down the corridor. Jeff hadn't seen him before. "What the hell are you making such a racket for?"

"I want to call my lawyer. I still haven't had my call."

"All right. Just stop wrecking the place." He looked into the cell, saw Wilson stretched out on the bench. "I'm surprised your new companion can sleep through this."

Jeff gave him a grin. "He told me he was very tired."

The guard unlocked the door and told Jeff to come out. "I'll have to put cuffs on you, though. Can't have you trying to escape, can we now?" He seemed jovial, almost friendly.

Maybe he doesn't know yet who I am. "Don't worry. I'd rather get out of here the legal way. It's safer." Jeff chuckled.

The guard took him into the front office. Jeff dialed the number on the card. Morgan answered on the second ring. "I'll take your offer," Jeff told him. "Can you get me out of this place? Today?"

After a slight pause Morgan said, "Let me talk to the officer on duty."

Jeff handed the phone to the guard. "My lawyer wants to talk to you."

Whatever Morgan told the officer seemed to have a sobering effect on him. He put down the phone and looked at Jeff. His face showed no expression. "You're supposed to wait here," he told Jeff.

"All right. No problem. I have no other plans," Jeff joked, but the guard stayed cool.

About half an hour later two burly marines walked in. One of them spoke to the officer.

"You are released into the custody of these guys. It is out of my hands now," the officer told Jeff. "Good luck."

"Who are they?"

"They say they're from Homeland Security."

"What? I'm not going with them. I'm waiting until my lawyer gets here," Jeff said angrily.

"Sorry. We have no jurisdiction over you. Not anymore." He shrugged.

The two marines waited until Jeff collected his possessions, and then they flanked him and marched him out of the building. A military van waited for them outside and they ordered Jeff to enter it. He contemplated running away but gave up that idea. Shrugging and resigning himself to the situation, he climbed into the rear of the van.

As his eyes adjusted to the semi-darkness of the interior, he saw a familiar figure sitting on a padded bench. The young man beamed at Jeff. "Hello, Lieutenant Chartrand."

"Rob? What the hell is going on?"

"We came to get you out."

"I don't quite understand."

The door connecting the rear of the van with the front cab opened and a heavy-set man stepped through. "Hello, Chartrand. I'm glad you've made your decision," Morgan said in his jovial tone. He joined Rob on the bench. "Take a seat. We are in a bit of a hurry to get away."

Jeff stared at Morgan. "Are you working for Homeland Security?"

"No, I don't." Morgan smiled slyly. "Let me introduce myself again, Lieutenant Chartrand. I'm Captain Elias Morgan."

"You're not a lawyer?"

"I am a lawyer. I work for Grey Ops." Morgan smiled. "Normally, I wouldn't reveal myself to you, but the Colonel suggested I do. We need you and you need us. As I told you, I am your life raft. Without me, without Grey Ops, you will surely disappear in the quagmire the guys from Homeland Security have driven you into. They want your blood." He stared at Jeff. "Why?"

Jeff shrugged. "I don't know, I thought you guys did."

Morgan shook his head. "For some unexplained reason even we can't seem to get any information and that's what worries us. Something big is brewing and we need to find out what. You seem to be in the middle of it."

Chapter Seventeen

"Since I am in the custody of the Military, does that mean I am under arrest?" Jeff stood at the window of the apartment and looked at the bleak scenery outside. He knew the building he was in was somewhere in an industrial area and the apartment in an abandoned warehouse.

"You are not under arrest, not even house-arrest. Whatever you do is up to you, Chartrand." Morgan heaved his bulk into one of the leather chairs and looked around the apartment. "This is not such a bad place to be stuck in. There is a fully equipped gym downstairs, at your disposal." He chuckled. "Wouldn't want you to go flabby…like me."

"How long do I have to stay cooped-up?"

Morgan shrugged. "I don't know. Once the cops find out it wasn't Homeland Security that sprung you, there'll be a nationwide manhunt for you. I'll be questioned, but I can tell them that the Military took you into custody for unspecified reasons. They hired my services merely as a negotiator. I only made the arrangements."

"What about the Military?" Jeff asked.

"Nobody will know anything." Morgan grinned. "It wouldn't be the first time somebody disappears without a trace. You should know about that."

Jeff gave Morgan a questioning look. "What has the Colonel told you about me?"

Morgan laughed, falling into the role of the jovial uncle again. "Whatever he has told me is safe with me, Lieutenant. Let me remind you that I am a Captain. I've been with Military Intelligence almost as long as Colonel Cowley. I can keep secrets. You know, I didn't always weigh over three hundred pounds. Before I decided to become a lawyer,

I was a field agent and I tipped the scales at around 185 pounds. I struck a mighty fine figure in those days, if I may say so."

Jeff smiled. "You don't look so bad now. I'll bet all that bulk is pure muscle."

Morgan sighed. "Don't try to flatter me, my friend. Let's face it I'm fat. Too much red meat, too many lobsters and too many beers." He studied Jeff. "You're lucky. You possess a great physique. Take my advice, don't ever let yourself go the way I did."

"How long have you been with Grey Ops?" Jeff asked, curious.

"Ever since its incubation."

"Then you must have been aware of most operations."

"All of them. Some of them I planned myself."

"Mine?"

He nodded. "You're no stranger to me, son."

"In other words you know everything about me?"

"Everything."

Jeff smirked. "You can have me put away for a long time. Maybe even have me court-martialed."

"I could, but I'm as guilty as you are. Don't forget that. Whatever we did had to be done, for the good of the country, maybe the world." Morgan didn't smile and Jeff knew the man meant what he said. Looking at his watch, Morgan said, "I'd better be going. I have a meeting tonight with a new client."

When Jeff lifted his eyebrow, Morgan smiled. "A legitimate one. After all, I am a lawyer in the real world."

"Before you go, I have one more question. What about food?"

"The fridge is stocked with fruit and vegetables. There are soft drinks and beer. No wine, I'm afraid." He gave Jeff an amused smile. "I don't think you'll have any romantic dinners for a while, but you'll have plenty to eat. TV dinners are in the freezer." Morgan rose. "You're not a prisoner, Chartrand. There'll be no guards outside, but you'd do well to stay out of sight. For your own safety." He reached into his pocket and pulled out a small cell phone. "Give me your phone."

Jeff hesitated. "All my contacts are in my phone."

"That's precisely why I want it. Don't contact anyone. You've disappeared. As of today you're a ghost."

Jeff knew Morgan was right. But knowing it didn't help. Barbara would be worried sick. After seeing his picture in the news, arrested and accused of all those terrible things, knowing she was partially responsible in the shooting of Galliano, didn't help.

Maxine would wonder and she'd suspect what happened.

He handed his phone to Morgan, took the one he was offered.

"This phone can't be traced, but use it only in an emergency," Morgan told him and walked toward the door. Before he walked out, he said, "There is a gun on the night table in the bedroom. You'll never know."

Jeff locked the door after him. He walked back to the window and stared at storm clouds that were beginning to gather in the darkening sky, promising a gloomy night. As gloomy as his mood.

A flash of lightening zigzagged between the dark swirling clouds, followed by another one. He didn't hear the thunder through the thick glass that kept him isolated from the outside, but he knew the system was still far away. It reminded him of his time as a child, growing up on his parent's farm. He remembered counting between the flash and the thunderclap to determine how close the thunderstorm was.

Being the oldest, he tried to convince Michael and Barbara that it was a secret not many knew about, a secret told to him by their Sioux grandmother, a secret only the eldest in the tribe would be allowed to know.

Barbara, the youngest of them, believed him, but Michael just laughed. "Everyone knows that. That's no big secret, you dummy."

Oh, Michael, if it weren't for you I would not be standing here, staring at these dark clouds.

Morgan had been correct. The freezer was full of frozen dinners. He popped one into the microwave oven and got himself a beer.

Wonder what Connie is up to right now? She'd miss him at the funeral; probably try to call him. Of course, she'd seen him on TV. If for some reason she hadn't, his face would be on every newspaper in the country by morning. MacKay would see to that. He'd be branded Enemy Number One.

His future looked bleak.

After the third beer, he felt a little better. Rain splattered against the window, but the expected thunderstorm never came. At least some things didn't turn bad, like every other thing these past few days.

Galliano, you son of a bitch! You deserved to be shot, but why did I have to be the one pulling the trigger? And why did Michael have to get involved with you?

His thoughts drifted to Kalila. She told him that Michael had been involved in illegal activities. Selling arms to terrorists? He still did not believe it. Not Michael! Of course, he was not the white sheep everyone thought; he had cheated on Samantha and fathered a child with another woman, who paid for that indiscretion with her life. Murdered by her own people, all because of their screwed-up beliefs.

What kind of world are we living in? What god would create a world of intolerance and hatred, where men strapped bombs around their bodies to kill themselves and innocent people they've never met? Just because some lunatic told them it was the right thing to do? A world in which a mother was proud to have a son who would do such an awful thing. A mother who was supposed to love that son, protect him from harm, not encourage him to go and kill himself.

What kind of mother would do that?

He had two more beers and fell asleep in his chair.

* * * *

The smell of frying bacon and eggs woke him up. Disoriented at first, he soon realized where he was. Throwing back the covers, he climbed out of bed and stretched, trying to get the kinks out of his neck muscles. Sleeping in a chair was not the ideal way to rest. Luckily, he woke up before his whole body stiffened up. He had spent at least part of the night in a comfortable bed.

He stuck his head out of the door, wondering who would be making breakfast for him.

"Good Morning, Lieutenant Chartrand. I hope you like your coffee black. Someone forgot to buy milk or cream."

Jeff blinked at the young man. "Hi, Rob. What are you doing here?"

"Making breakfast."

"I can see that. How can you be so cheerful this early in the morning?" Jeff rubbed his eyes. "I appreciate this, but it would have been nicer to have a woman wake me up, preferably with a kiss," he said with a grin.

"Well, I can't help you there." Rob chuckled. "But maybe I can have it arranged for next time. Hurry up and take your shower before your breakfast gets cold."

Jeff threw up his hands. "Who needs a woman when I have you? You sound just like one. I think you'll make a good house-husband some day."

"No chance of that. When I get married my wife will serve me."

"Good luck with that. Women these days are much too independent. You'll be serving her." Jeff laughed and headed for the bathroom.

He felt much better after his shower and he joined Rob at the table. Breakfast tasted good and it put him in an even better mood.

Rob poured himself another coffee. "I told you that you'd be working for us again," he said.

"Yeah," Jeff growled. "But not by choice. I'd hoped I left all that behind when I was discharged after being wounded."

"My dad, the Colonel, always says once you work for Grey Ops you can never really leave." Rob laughed. "You've strayed from your true destiny, but now you've come back home."

Jeff let his eyes wander around the apartment. "Isn't a home supposed to feel like…well…a home?" he asked.

"Yes. Why? You don't feel at home here?"

"Not really, but it seems I'll have to get used to this place. By the way, what is your real reason for being here, Rob? Aside from making breakfast."

"Captain Morgan suggested I be your sparring partner. Maybe you can teach me a few tricks?"

"I doubt that," Jeff said thoughtfully. "If you work for Grey Ops you must have some qualifications that set you apart from the rest."

Rob shrugged. "I'm sort of a computer whiz. But then, so is every other kid these days."

"You're not a kid. Not at twenty-five. Not in the army, even if you look like one. When I was your age I was deeply involved in covert operations."

"I never said I wasn't," Rob said, smiling. Suddenly, he looked ten years older.

After breakfast, Rob suggested they try out the gym. The place was a surprise to Jeff. Large enough for a dozen people to exercise. There was even a punch bag and a mat for martial arts practice. He found a pair of gloves that fit his big fists and punched the bag a few times. "You box?" he asked Rob.

The young man nodded. "A little."

"How about going a couple of rounds?"

"Sure."

Jeff got another surprise when he saw Rob in boxer shorts. The sloppy clothes he wore had been hiding his physique. He wasn't large but his body was covered with corded muscles.

Rob looked at Jeff with appreciation showing clearly in his face, but he didn't comment. He turned out to be quite an excellent boxer and delivered some hard punches.

"Let's see what you can do with martial arts," Jeff said after going a few rounds.

Rob gave him a quick smile and went to look for a couple of uniforms. "It helps me to focus when I wear my gi," he explained.

The uniforms had gray belts. "Everyone who practices here has a black belt, but we don't care about degrees," he said to Jeff, "that's why all the belts are gray, but you probably know that."

"Twenty years ago we didn't practice in fancy gyms like this one," Jeff said, "and we wore only army fatigue."

Rob came across as a mild-mannered young man, but on the mat, he changed into an aggressive opponent, attacking Jeff without warning. Only Jeff's quick reflexes saved him from a kick to the head. He felt tired but content after the workout. Maybe being cooped-up in this place wouldn't be as bad as he feared. Not with a sparring partner like Rob.

Chapter Eighteen

When Colonel Cowley walked through the door, Jeff knew by his somber expression that something was wrong.

"Good to see you," Cowley said, giving Jeff a salute.

Surprised, Jeff returned the salute, something he had not done since his discharge from the army sixteen years ago. "Good to see you also, Colonel." He indicated a chair, waited until Cowley seated himself until he continued, "I have a feeling you didn't come here to chat."

"No, I haven't." Cowley put the briefcase he carried onto the table. "How are you doing so far?"

Jeff smiled. "Well, three weeks without being able to go outside, almost makes me feel I'm in a prison. Comfortable, yes, but still a prison."

"I understand, but it couldn't be helped. After all, this had to be done to keep you out of a real prison."

"I know and I'm not complaining, but this inactivity is driving me insane. I still need to find out the circumstances of my brother's murder. The more time passes the faster the evidence will fade away."

Cowley pulled a CD out of his briefcase. "You might want to watch this one."

Jeff popped the CD into the player and turned on the television.

The picture on the screen showed four men wearing black hoods and facemasks. Three carried machine guns, one held a long knife. Across the bottom of the screen flashed a string of characters. Jeff couldn't read them, but he knew they were Arabic.

Then two more masked men walked into the scene. Between them, they held a small child. A boy. Possibly three years old. He didn't struggle or cry, but he appeared frightened as he looked around with large eyes.

The camera focused on his face.

Jeff almost cursed when he saw the blue eyes.

As the face of the boy faded away, the camera showed a close-up shot of the man with the knife. He spoke with a harsh voice, slashing the air with his knife. "If our demands are not met we will cut the throat of this spawn of an American infidel dog and spill his blood in the name of Allah."

The man put the edge of the keen blade against the little boy's neck and made sawing motions. "We will ship his head in a box to America. The sword of Allah has already taken vengeance and claimed the blood of his father. Allah is great!"

Jeff didn't listen to the rest of the message. His head suddenly spinning, he didn't have to ask who this little boy was. "Where did you get this?" he asked with a voice gone dry.

"This was recorded from the internet just yesterday," Colonel Cowley explained quietly.

"Why show it to me?" Jeff asked.

"Because this message was meant for you."

"For me?" He asked the question, even though knowing that Cowley spoke the truth.

"This is your brother's son, Jeff," the Colonel said gently.

Jeff stared at the screen, at the scared face of the little boy, at the large blue eyes—the eyes of his brother, Michael. "Those fucking heartless sons of bitches!" he cursed. "He's just an innocent little child." He looked at Cowley. "What are their demands?"

The Colonel shrugged. "They never said, but I'm sure you know what they want, don't you?"

Something suddenly popped into Jeff's head. A question. "How do you know this is my brother's son? I only found out just recently that Michael had a child with an Iraqi girl. Where did you get your information?"

Cowley smiled. "Are you forgetting who we are, Lieutenant? You've been away far too long." His eyes rested on Jeff. "You know they'll kill him, even if you meet their demands."

Jeff nodded, his gaze flicking back to the frozen face on the screen.

Michael, how the hell could you do this? Why couldn't you keep that prick of yours in your pants?

"We have two weeks," Cowley said. "Enough time to mount a rescue mission."

"You don't even know where they are holding him."

"We will find out. You were complaining about being inactive, Chartrand. This will be your first mission. It'll take you out of the country. You'll be safer in Iraq than in the States."

Jeff looked sharply at the Colonel. "I don't know how you found out about my brother's son, but if you did, others might have and I'm not talking about these Iraqi kidnappers."

Cowley nodded in agreement. "I'm sure they have, but Homeland Security, the FBI and the CIA have no interest in saving this little boy's life. His death might even help their cause."

"Those kidnappers mentioned my brother's murder, giving 'The sword of Allah' credit for his death. Do you think they murdered Michael?"

"I don't know. It is possible."

"If they did then I will want to find them," Jeff said grimly. "Maybe you're right. We should try and rescue that boy..." He paused and added, "...my nephew."

Cowley smiled and nodded. "I'd figured you'd be interested. I'll put together a team. Give me a couple of days. Until then I want you to watch these videos from Iraq and familiarize yourself with the country, the present political situation, and the locations of known terrorist groups." He pulled out a stack of CDs. "I'll contact you again in two days."

Rising, he held out a hand. "Welcome back to Grey Ops, Lieutenant."

After the Colonel left, he watched the video with the kidnappers again, studying the face of the boy.

"Omar Chartrand," he whispered. "We'll get you home. Alive. I promise you that."

* * * *

He spent the day studying the CDs Cowley left with him.

When he watched the news on television that evening, he didn't find any mention of the kidnapping.

Probably not newsworthy, he thought.

The next morning he exercised alone. Rob hadn't shown up for two days now and Jeff wondered why. He was just going through a series of martial arts moves, when he heard the opening of the door that led into the gym. A slim figure, dressed in a black bodysuit stepped into the room.

Female, judging by the curvy body. A skullcap covered her head and face; only her eyes showed like two black, glittering gems through small slits in the mask.

She didn't say anything as she joined him on the mat. Giving him a slight bow, she fell into a classic stance. Then, without warning, she attacked him, reminding him a little of Rob. He parried the move and, within moments, they were engaged in a mock fight.

Grudgingly, he had to admit that she was exceptionally good, giving him a nice workout. She moved and struck like a cobra, even hissing loudly when she attacked.

They ended the match when she jumped back and bowed to him.

"How about taking off that mask and let me see who made me sweat this morning," he said, grinning.

With a quick movement, she removed the mask and smiled at him.

"Kalila," he burst out in surprise. "How did you get in here and how did you know I was here?"

She laughed. "Through that door, but do not worry, I did not come to assassinate you. Had I wanted to do that, you would be dead now." Then she became serious. "Colonel Cowley had me dropped off. I will be keeping you company for a while. We are supposed to get to know each other better."

"You mean you're going to move in with me?" he asked.

She nodded.

"Why?"

"Because I am a member of the team that is going to rescue Omar." When she saw his perplexed expression, she asked, "Do you have a problem working with a female partner?"

"Never have, but this is different."

"How so?"

"This will be a dangerous mission. You could get killed."

"So could you," she countered.

"I'm a soldier. I was trained for missions like this one."

She laughed softly. "So was I. Besides, you will need me. I will be in familiar territory. I can protect you."

"I don't need a woman to protect me," he said, almost angrily. "I can take care of myself."

"You talk like an Iraqi man," she said, contempt clearly in her voice. "Iraqi men do not think much of women either."

"Don't compare me with them. I'm an American. I treat women with respect. I protect them. I don't have much use for a man who beats his wife or daughters." Now he was angry.

She glared at him. "Well, then what is your problem? Just pretend I am a weak woman and you are protecting me." She walked up to him and touched his biceps. "You look big and strong; I do not doubt that you can protect a woman with those big muscles." She flashed him a big smile.

"Are you sure you are an Iraqi?" he asked. "As I already told you before, you don't talk or act like an oppressed woman."

"I was never married and my father always gave my mother the respect she deserved. Not every Iraqi man is abusive." Her dark eyes studied him silently. "The fact is you will never be able to locate anyone in Iraq without someone who knows the people and the customs. As an American, you will be obvious wherever you go. I assume you do not speak the language. I do. I will teach you everything you need to know. I will teach you how to blend in without being noticed."

She looked into his face. "You have black hair and I can see the dark stubble on your chin. How fast can you grow a beard?"

"My facial hair grows pretty quickly. It's my French ancestry, I guess."

"Good. Starting today, you will stop shaving."

"You are serious, aren't you?" Seeing her standing in front of him in her tight bodysuit that revealed every detail of her slim but curvy body, her face still a little flushed from the workout, he felt a sudden strong sexual attraction toward her.

Damn! That's all I needed. He wore only boxer shorts and the material wasn't very thick. "There is something I need to have clarified," he said, to cover up his embarrassment. "What is your connection with Colonel Cowley?"

She gave him an impish smile. "I am a double agent. I work for Grey Ops."

Jeff took a moment to digest that information. Then he said, "I guess that's how the Colonel found out who that kidnapped little boy is."

"Correct. I told him." Her face stayed serious. "You must have wondered a little why Grey Ops would get involved in the rescue of an obscure child."

"The question occurred to me."

"Because I begged Colonel Cowley. He was not enthusiastic about it, but I told him that I would be willing to go and I wanted you on the team. It did not take him too long to decide, since he liked the idea that it would get you out of the country for a while."

"I thought your reason for being in America was to find the illegal arms dealers."

"It still is. That has not changed, but rescuing Omar is of greater importance to me. He is the only thing I have left of my sister." Her big dark eyes looked into his. "He is part of you also. Your family's blood flows in his veins."

"If your sister was as beautiful as you, I can see why my brother fell in love with her," Jeff said slowly. He lifted his hand to touch her cheek but restrained himself from doing so, smoothing back his hair instead.

If she noticed the slight hesitation of his hand, she didn't show it. Smiling, she said, "I would like to take a shower and then I want to move my stuff into our suite. I hope there is a second bedroom."

"There is, but only one bathroom." He grinned lopsidedly, feeling like an awkward schoolboy in her presence. The faces of Maxine and Connie popped into his mind. Two different people, two different personalities. He liked Maxine for her cool, attractive appearance and her independent strong character. Connie for her exotic looks and great passion. This woman was so different from both of them. She had a haunting beauty about her and shown fierce passion when they faced each other on the mat.

I wonder how she is in bed. Wouldn't mind taming this hellcat.

He turned away, feeling uneasy because of his thoughts. "There is a shower down here. I'm taking it. You can use the one in the suite," he told her as he walked toward the changing room. He knew she was watching him, probably wondering why he acted so brash. The last thing he needed was for her to see him reacting sexually to her presence.

Hearing her soft laughter, he had a feeling she was aware of her effect on him and of his discomfort.

This was not an oppressed woman!

Her reaction did not help at all.

After his shower, he dressed and went upstairs. He saw a duffle bag on the chesterfield in the living room; it obviously belonged to Kalila. When he walked past the bathroom, he heard the shower.

I hope she's not in the habit of walking around naked, like me.

Dammit! He had to control his thoughts. If they were going to go on a mission together, he could not afford to let sexual tension come between them. Under different circumstances, he would probably make a play for her, but this was not the right time or place.

He went back into the living room and turned on the TV, and then he popped in one of the CDs about Iraq.

When she came into the room, she wore a light coat. He could see her shapely body outlined against the window underneath the flimsy material. Her black hair was still wet and hung in strands around her face and down her shoulders, making her incredibly attractive. The way she looked at him, he had the distinct feeling she was trying to tease him.

Looking at the screen, she smiled and said, "I see, you are trying to familiarize yourself with my country. That is a good thing."

"Like you said, I'm trying," he said. "How useful this information is, I don't really know."

"Whatever you find on those CDs is probably biased because it was put together by Americans. You will do better with what I can teach you." She sat down beside him and crossed her legs inside her coat. He merely saw them up to her knees and, as he suspected, they were slim and beautifully formed.

She probably has great strong thighs.

"Am I making you nervous?" she asked.

He cleared his throat, which suddenly felt dry. "I don't think I have to answer that. You are an attractive woman. Very sexy, too, especially at this moment. And I'm a virile man at best. You're not making it easy for me."

"If we are to work together we have to be comfortable with each other," she said. "Our lives may depend on it." She hooded her eyes, gave him a look that did not make him comfortable. "I admit I was attracted to you from the first time I talked with you in the restaurant. And I still am, but we must not let that influence our conduct. That is the reason we have to live together for a while before we go on this mission." She smiled. "Once we get used to each other the tension will ease. We will be just like an old married couple."

"We're not married," he said with a somewhat crooked grin.

"But you were once. I never was." She rose, smoothed out her coat. Then she grabbed her duffle bag. "I will put this away."

"Is that all you have?" he asked.

"No. My suitcase is already in my room. Where did you think I got this coat from?"

He shrugged. "I was never in that bedroom. I don't know what's in the closet."

"No skeletons, I can assure you of that," she said, chuckling.

"I'm curious. How did you know I was married?" He tried hard not to stare at her nipples poking against the thin fabric.

"I always make sure I know everything about the people I work with."

"Then you have the advantage. I know very little about you, except for the stuff you told me. And I don't even know if everything you told me is actually true."

He could have looked at her forever, the almost regal way she carried her body, the way she tilted her head when she watched him out of her dark, haunting eyes. And she had the most beautiful smile, especially when she seemed to mock him a little.

The way she did at this moment.

"Is a mysterious woman not more exciting, Jeff? The less you know about me, the more you will want to get to know me." She shook strands of hair out of her eyes; a movement that sent shivers down his spine. "Maybe when this is over I will let you find out everything you will want to know, but until then be satisfied with what you get. Colonel Cowley will vouch for me, in case you are worried I might be a spy or an assassin. And as I already pointed out, we are practically related." She hurried away toward her bedroom, moving gracefully across the carpet on bare feet.

He sighed, watching her. Life did not seem fair. Ten years of nothing, and now he was involved with two beautiful women and attracted to a third one. One who was most likely to turn his whole world upside down.

The stuff he was watching on the screen didn't seem that important anymore. Kalila was right. She'd be a bigger asset and more valuable than any information he could gather from these CDs.

Checking his watch, he noticed that it was close to noon. Might as well start lunch. He didn't know what Kalila ate and he hoped there was something in the freezer for her. As he began rummaging around in the freezer, someone knocked on the door; it opened and Rob walked in, carrying a large box.

"Well, well," Jeff said. "Look who the wind blew in."

Rob grinned and set the box on the table in the kitchen. "I'm told you have a guest." He winked. "A female guest. I brought some food for her."

Jeff smirked. "No need to wink, my young friend. She is not the female companion I requested from you." Looking at the box, he said, "I assume you know who she is. What kind of goodies did you bring for her?"

"There is some yogurt, rice, olives, milk and cheese. Also some frozen lamb chops, some chicken and some beef cubes." He shrugged. "I'm told her people like grilled meats, but we can't supply you with a BBQ. The oven will have to do. I also brought a bunch of different spices."

"Who do you think is going to prepare that stuff?" Jeff asked.

"I guess I will have to do that," Kalila said from the doorway into the kitchen. She smiled at Rob. "Kind of you to think of my special preferences, but I could have adjusted to the American food Jeff is eating."

Rob waved it off. "Orders from the Colonel. He wants you to feel at home here. I'm sure you'd return the favor would we be in your country."

"Your people already are in my country," Kalila said and, looking at Jeff, "I will try to make you feel welcome when you are in Iraq, but I am afraid there will not be much time for socializing."

Jeff was surprised to see her in jeans and a checkered shirt, but she still looked attractive, especially with her long hair tied into a ponytail. She reminded him a lot of Nicole who loved to pin back her hair just like that. She had the same figure and even a little of Nicole's attitude.

Thinking of Nicole brought back pangs of guilt. How could he ever love another woman again when her memory kept stirring up feelings he tried so hard to suppress? Feelings of remorse for not insisting she stay home that night and for letting her drive alone in a thunderstorm on a dark highway made slippery by a blanket of hail.

"Something wrong?" Kalila's voice sounded concerned. "You look…ah…strange."

He swallowed, shook his head. "No," he said. "Just a ghost from a long time ago. Nothing to worry about." He smiled. "You look ravishing."

Her hand moved to her face to push back a strand of black hair that wouldn't stay out of her eyes. "Do I look American?" she asked, smiling impishly.

"Very much so," he said, but then he grinned. "Now all you have to do is lose your accent."

"I like her accent," Rob chimed in and looked at Kalila. "It makes you sound exotic, mysterious."

Kalila laughed. "Are all American men always trying to seduce a woman by giving her compliments?"

Rob gave her a wolfish grin. "Not all, just me and Lieutenant Chartrand here." His gaze flicked to Jeff. "Sorry, Lieutenant, I didn't mean to imply anything."

Jeff didn't mind the playful bantering. It kept him from thinking about things he didn't want to worry about. He kept seeing the face of Omar, kept seeing the fear in the little boy's blue eyes. There was a sudden urgency in him. He needed to get out, see some action, before he went stir crazy. Going to Iraq would not be a picnic, far from it, but it was his duty to Michael to try to save his son. The only son keeping his brother's memory and name alive.

"It's all right, Rob. I know you're only kidding. You are far too young to even look at a beautiful lady like Miss Ahmed." He gave Rob a little smile. "By the way, where have you been these last few days? I missed your company."

Rob shrugged. "I have other things to do than cook for you, Lieutenant," he said, chuckling.

"Like what?"

"That is classified information. You'll have to get clearance from the Colonel first, before I can tell you," Rob said with a whisper. He put his finger in front of his mouth. "Besides, this apartment might be bugged." He smiled, but his eyes didn't.

Jeff had never given it any thought, but then he began to realize that he had lost some of his touch. In the old days, he would never have overlooked that possibility.

"Who would bug this apartment?" he asked, given his voice a light, joking tone.

"Who knows? These days, with all the electronic gadgets available, everything is possible. You'll find cameras on traffic lights and on many street corners, on government and on private buildings. We are being watched, wherever we are." Rob lowered his voice confidentially. "Somebody might be watching us right now."

He broke into sudden laughter. "Don't worry, this place is secure. I swept it myself before you moved in. There are no hidden cameras or microphones. Your phone is not bugged and neither is the computer. This place is a sanctuary for people who want to disappear for a while. So relax."

He said it, but Jeff knew he had been warned.

Rob looked at his watch. "How time flies. It's past noon, time to get a bite to eat. I hate eating by myself, so if you don't mind, I'll prepare something and we can have an intimate dinner, just the three of us. What do you say?"

"Fine by me, unless Miss Ahmed objects to having a threesome," Jeff said, grinning at the young man's enthusiasm.

Kalila laughed softly and shook her head. "My American is good enough to understand what a threesome really means, but if you mean just eating together, I have no objections."

"Well, then we are in business." Rob rubbed his hands. "I'll make us three lamb chops with fried rice, and I'll even throw in some olives and raisins. And for desert a small bowl of rice pudding." He reached into the box and pulled out a bottle of wine. "Merlot. This will go perfectly with it."

"No wine for me," Kalila said. "Just some fruit juice, if you have."

"Your wish is my command, my Lady." Rob made a little bow. "That leaves more wine for the Lieutenant and me."

"Are you even old enough to drink?" Jeff joked.

"Barely," Rob said, grinning.

"I can help you with the cooking," Kalila said. "I am a very good cook."

"I don't doubt that, but you just sit back and relax and let me do all the work. Once I'm gone, you can cook all you want."

"I think I am going to like it here," Kalila said, smiling. "Being served by a man will be a welcome change for me."

Chapter Nineteen

The next few days went by faster than Jeff would have liked. Kalila proved to be a pleasant companion and a great cook, even though much of the stuff they ate came from frozen dinners. However, Kalila insisted Rob bring some fresh vegetables and fruit, including lots of yogurt and unfrozen lamb and beef. And freshly baked bread. Some of the stuff she cooked didn't agree with Jeff's palate, like raisins and olives in his salad. He was a meat and potato man. Sugar and salt didn't mix. Not in his book.

They practiced every day on the mat. Kalila began to wear the traditional gi when sparring, instead of the bodysuit she wore when they sparred for the first time, and Jeff didn't mind. It kept him from being distracted by her curvy body.

The rest of the time, she kept him busy with facts about Iraq and the way of life there. He found most of it fascinating. Iraq was a beautiful country, but the constant wars had changed much of the way of life. Ever since the American Invasion and the capture of Saddam Hussein, who reigned with an iron fist and kept the people under control, the sectarian wars were tearing the country apart. Bombings were a daily occurrence and most people were unhappy.

She didn't keep it a secret that the Iraqi people wanted the American invaders out. However, she admitted things would only get worse, unless the Iraqi government could gain control over all factions. Unfortunately, this would only mean another form of dictatorship.

Jeff refrained from making too many statements, aware of the warning Rob had given him. He didn't know who would be keeping taps on their conversations, especially since his presence here was supposed to be a secret, but he learned a long time ago caution was much better than hindsight. It never hurt to be a little bit paranoid, not when you were in the kind of business Jeff seemed to be involved in once again.

Rob showed up a couple of times just to say hello, but otherwise they were left to themselves.

Colonel Cowley made an appearance exactly six days after Kalila moved into the apartment. "I see you two have not killed each other," he said when he walked through the door. "I guess you might even form a good team."

"Good to see you, too, Colonel Cowley," Kalila said, giving him a questioning look. "Any news from the kidnappers?"

Cowley shook his head in denial. "We haven't heard from them, but our sources in Iraq tell us a group that calls itself The Needle of Allah is holed up somewhere in a small town near Al Kut. Apparently, this group is heavily involved in supplying arms to other terrorists." He smiled grimly. "You know, even in Iraq there are some people who do not like to see a little boy used as a hostage."

"When are we leaving?" Kalila asked, trying unsuccessfully to hide her anxiety.

Cowley looked at Jeff. "You can leave whenever you feel you're ready. I don't want to pressure you, but I believe time is of the essence."

"I'm as ready as I'll ever be," Jeff said.

"Good, then you'll leave tomorrow. I'll have Rob pick you up at six hundred hours. A support team is already on standby." He gave Jeff a look of approval. "I notice you're growing a beard. That is good. It won't make you stand out." He smiled. "You already look like an Iraqi."

"It was Miss Ahmed's idea," Jeff said. "The credit goes to her."

* * * *

The team consisted of eight people, Jeff and Kalila included. Jeff was surprised to see Rob among the team.

"When did you find out you were coming with us?" Jeff asked him.

Rob grinned. "From the beginning. You didn't think I'd stay behind, did you, Lieutenant?"

"I didn't give it any thought, to be honest." Jeff studied the young man. He still looked like an enthusiastic schoolboy, even with his newly acquired mustache, but Jeff knew there was more hidden behind Rob's open face and smiling eyes than just simple enthusiasm. "I hope you won't be a burden and slow us down," he said jokingly, glad to see at least one familiar face, but at the same time he worried about Rob's welfare. "By the way, you don't look too bad with that mustache. I'm surprised it's this thick." He grinned. "I didn't even know you had to shave already."

Rob chuckled. "I'm disappointed. I thought you knew me better than that, Lieutenant."

He looked over the rest of the team. All were young, mid-twenties, except for one of them, a slender tall man with a dark complexion, black hair and bushy eyebrows. Jeff judged him to be in his early thirties.

"I'm Sergeant Abduk," the man said when he noticed Jeff scrutinizing him.

"You look Arabic," Jeff observed.

The sergeant grinned. "So do you, sir."

"I'm not, just look like one. Once the beard is off my appearance will change. I'm an American."

"So am I, sir. Born and raised in Kentucky."

"But your parents were not, right?"

"No, sir, they weren't. They came to America thirty-five years ago from Samarra."

"That's in Iraq."

"Correct, sir. Is that a problem?"

"No problem, Sergeant." Jeff wondered why the man had been chosen. His appearance and name could not have been the only reason. "Do you speak Iraqi?" he asked.

"Like a native." Abduk grinned. "My parents taught me."

"Are you a Muslim, Sergeant Abduk?"

"No, sir. I'm Catholic. That was the reason why my parents left Iraq. They felt persecuted in Iraq."

Jeff let out a silent sigh of relief. Having one Muslim, Kalila, on the team was enough. He didn't need a member of his team taking time out five times a day to bow east and pray. He realized he was being prejudiced, but that was the way he felt. He didn't care for fanatics, no matter what religion or belief.

They assembled inside a small room on the military base. Every man carried his pack and a sidearm. Again, it was Sergeant Abduk who seemed to be the exception. He wasn't armed. Instead, he had a camera hanging around his neck.

"Are you planning to take pictures in Iraq?" Jeff asked.

"Lots of them," the sergeant confirmed. "That will be my cover on this mission. I'll be a newspaper photographer." He gave Jeff his big smile. "Used to be my job before I joined the army."

"I knew there was more to you than just a pretty face," Jeff said, beginning to like the man. He was about to have the others introduce themselves, when the door opened and Colonel Cowley walked in.

All stood at attention, including Jeff. Old habits were taking over. The years seemed to fall away. He was forty-two, the oldest member of the team, but he felt confident he could keep up with any of them.

"Good morning, men," Cowley said, and then he looked at Kalila. "And Miss Ahmed."

She nodded and gave him a little smile. Even though she was dressed in army garb, Jeff still found her attractive. More so now than ever, after spending a week having her around him every minute of the day, and getting to know her.

"I see you're all ready to leave. I don't have to tell you this mission is going to be dangerous. Some of you may not come back, even though I hope you do. All of you have been briefed, but our information is at best sketchy. You will be going into territory not controlled by American Forces. You'll be on your own."

He paused. "You'll be taking a transport plane delivering supplies to Baghdad, where you'll be met by Colonel Settler. He's the only one who knows about your true mission. As far as anyone else is concerned, you're in Iraq on a reconnaissance mission, to gather special information. Lieutenant Chartrand is the investigator, Sergeant Abduk the cameraman, and Miss Ahmed the interpreter."

He looked at Rob. "Specialist Masters, you'll record the events. I want to have a detailed report on my desk upon your return. Understood?"

Rob saluted smartly. "Yes sir. Loud and clear. I'll to my best."

Cowley's gaze rested on him somewhat longer than necessary. Jeff could see the concern in the Colonel's eyes.

I didn't think the old man cared about anything but the army. I guess sending your only son into unknown danger worries even the man everyone used to call the Iron Gun.

Cowley looked at the other four soldiers. "Specialists Harmon, Hung, Armano, and Springer. You're job is to protect the news team."

"Yes, sir, Colonel," they said in unison.

He looked at Jeff. "Lieutenant, you will receive your file in Baghdad from Colonel Settler. And now I wish you all good luck. Your plane leaves in two hours."

"One last question, Colonel," Jeff said. "Are any of these men not Grey Ops?"

"None. They've been handpicked by me. They're the best, Lieutenant." He left without a backward glance.

Jeff checked his watch. "We have thirty minutes until we'll board the bus that'll take us to the airport. Enough time to become acquainted with each other."

* * * *

Traveling in a transport plane is not nearly as comfortable as traveling in a plane designed for passengers. No flight attendant came around to ask if they wanted something to drink or eat.

Jeff rummaged in his pack and pulled out a bottle filled with water. Taking a few swigs, he studied Rob, who sat across from him, writing something into a notebook. "Taking notes already?" he asked.

Rob looked up and grinned. "We've been in the air now for exactly five hours. Much has happened since we left."

Jeff chuckled. "You must have been in a different plane all this time. My butt is getting sore from sitting. By the way, I notice you're taking notes the old-fashioned way. Was there no money left for an electronic recording device?"

"I have those, too, but I still prefer paper and pen. More reliable. Battery-powered devices have a tendency to fail at the most inappropriate times."

"I see. I'm just surprised, because young people these days rely too much on their mp3 players, iPods, and multi-usage phones."

Rob shrugged. "I'm not like most young people," he said.

"I've noticed. You're an old wise man stuck inside a young body."

"If that's a compliment, I'll take it, Lieutenant." Rob went back to his scribbler and Jeff wondered what went on in the young man's head. His gaze traveled over to Sergeant Abduk, who sat busying himself doing crossword puzzles. The other four men sat on the floor playing cards.

"Sergeant Abduk, how long have you been with Grey Ops?"

Abduk looked up from his puzzles. "Eight years, sir."

"And before that?"

"Regular army, sir. Did six months in Bosnia in 1996."

"You're married, Sergeant?"

"Yes, sir. To a beautiful Blonde. Got two kids. A boy and a girl."

"Any of your missions ever take you to Iraq? You don't have to answer that unless you want to."

Abduk's eyes seemed to veil over for a moment, and then he said, "Not Iraq. Afghanistan. 2002. That's all I can tell you, sir."

"That's all right. It means you know what it's like in the desert."

"Yes, I do. All too well. Question, sir?"

"Go ahead."

"You've been in the Middle East?"

"1991. Gulf War. I was wounded there. January 29, a day I'll never forget. Most members of my unit died that day." Memory flooded back painfully.

Lieutenant Bernard, Ray Tremmer, Jesus Gomez, and Jerry Geisel.

Four good men.

They never knew that he was Grey Ops, sent there to spy on them. The reason for that didn't matter anymore.

He was the only one who made it back alive. Wounded but alive.

They promoted him to lieutenant before they discharged him. Even gave him a medal. He never knew why. The medal was collecting dust inside his closet.

"How?"

"Pardon me?" Jeff had barely heard Abduk ask the question.

"How did they die?"

"Our tent received a direct hit. It was a miracle I survived." The physical wounds had healed, but the memory of that day kept haunting him. Mostly in his dreams.

"Tough," Abduk said. "I lost a couple of good friends in Afghanistan. Roadside bombs. It's a dirty war, sir. Those Muslims have no honor, especially the Taliban."

"I am a Muslim," Kalila said quietly beside Jeff.

176

Abduk's dark eyes rested on her. "My grandparents were Muslims. My parents became Catholics because they could not find it in their hearts to follow the teachings of a religion that does not treat women with equality. Let me ask you something. Do you hide your face behind a piece of cloth and wear dresses that cover your ankles when you are in Iraq?"

"Yes, I do, but only because I fear for my life should I walk around otherwise. It was not always like this in Iraq or Iran."

"I know, but it is like that now, because your clergy are all fanatics. Nowhere is it written in the Qur'an that a woman must wear a veil. That law was written by men and not by the Prophet." Abduk spoke quietly, but Jeff could tell this was a topic dear to his heart.

"The Bible was written by men," Kalila said.

"Yes, it was. The Old Testament tells the history of the Jews and the New Testament was written by the disciples of Jesus."

"So they say." Kalila smiled. "I am not ignorant about the teachings of the Bible. Neither am I ignorant about the history of the last two thousand years. The Catholic Church has not exactly been peaceful. It has split into a multitude of different groups, all basically believing the same thing. Many wars have been fought over religion and many people have been murdered in the name of God."

"Christians never strapped bombs to their bodies and walked into a crowd of innocent people to commit suicide."

"No, they would rather push a button to drop a bomb that destroys much of a whole city and kills over a hundred thousand civilians with one giant explosion and lets the survivors suffer for the rest of their lives because they have been exposed to deadly radiation," Kalila said vehemently.

"If you're referring to the atomic bombs that were dropped on Hiroshima and Nagasaki you are correct. Nobody really foresaw the terrible force those bombs released. It was a mistake. It must never happen again."

"It should not have happened the first time. Many people who study history wonder why they dropped the second bomb on Nagasaki three days after the first one if the Military of the US did not know the damage one atomic bomb can inflict."

Abduk shrugged. "I'm not a history buff and I don't know the answer to that question. You'd have to ask the generals and the politicians who were running the country in 1945. We've learned since then and we know we must not allow countries like Iraq, Iran, or North Korea have atomic weapons."

"I agree. I also think nobody should have any Weapons of Mass destruction." Kalila's smile seemed innocent, but Jeff detected the sarcasm. "Iraq never had them, even though your CIA insisted we did. Either someone fed your spy agencies wrong information or your government was purposely misled by the very people who are supposed to safeguard your country."

Abduk held up a hand. "I'm not going to comment on that, because now we're entering an area of abundant rumors and conspiracy theories."

"They may be rumors, but you know what they say. Where there is smoke there is fire. One thing is for certain, though…Iraq does not have these weapons but America has."

"That is true and it is a good thing. We have to defend our way of life and our freedom against the people who want to take it away from us and force their way of life on us. America does not want to dominate the world."

"No?" Kalila chuckled. "I believe now I am not going to comment."

"Are you two finished with your lover's quarrel?" Rob asked, looking up from his notebook. "I can't write as fast as you're talking."

"No lover's quarrel, just a friendly discussion," Kalila said. She threw Jeff a sidelong glance. "You have not said anything, Lieutenant Chartrand."

"I'm staying out of that, Miss Ahmed." Jeff gave her a friendly smile and shook his head. "I've heard way too many conspiracy theories from my own relatives. Every time we get together, I have to listen to them discussing things they know nothing about. Thank God, that doesn't happen too often." He looked at Rob. "I hope you were kidding when you made that remark about you can't write fast enough. Not everything that is said on this mission among the team needs to be repeated to outsiders."

Rob stopped writing. "Understood, Lieutenant. Besides, I was kidding." He grinned. "I figured somebody needs to joke every now and then. Is that allowed?"

"When it's appropriate and as long as it doesn't interfere with the mission, Specialist Masters." Jeff smiled to take away the edge from his comment. He needed to relax and loosen up. Nothing would be gained by becoming rigid and unbendable. Discipline was necessary within the Military, but it need not be a way of life. Not anymore, not for him.

He hated this whole business he had fallen into. His life as a cop had been satisfactory and mostly stress-free for the last few years. He thought he was finally getting over Nicole and could maybe, just maybe, start living again. Fuck it! Why did this have to happen with Michael?

His sudden anger must have shown in his posture, because Kalila turned to him and gave him a quizzing look. "Everything all right, Lieutenant Chartrand? Did you finally discover something we said that you do not agree with?"

"Nothing either of you said. Those are your opinions and it is not my place to judge and scrutinize what you're saying." He smiled at her. "I have my own issues I need to come to grips with. I am apprehensive about this mission and the fate of Omar. What if we can't find him in time?"

She put her hand on his in a gesture that implied intimacy, then spoke with a low voice, "I am as concerned as you are, Jeff. Remember, he is my nephew, also. We will find him, do not worry."

Her hand felt warm on his and he didn't pull away. He suddenly realized he was not alone. She may be an Iraqi, a possible enemy, with a different background, different views on life, but she was a woman. A woman with feelings no different from his. A woman he felt attracted to.

"Thank you, Kalila," he said, softly, so only she could hear, but he knew the others had not missed this small show of intimacy. They were trained to notice those things, just as he had been. Their survival could depend on seeing and knowing subtle things like that.

You needed to know your enemies as well as your friends. He didn't care what they thought and leaned back, closing his eyes. It wouldn't hurt to get some shuteye.

End of Book One
To be continued in Book Two
Traitors and Patriots

Look for Web of Conspiracy books 2 & 3 by Herbert Grosshans, coming soon from www. mélange-books.com.

Check out other great read at Melange-Books!

www.ingramcontent.com/pod-product-compliance
Lightning Source LLC
Chambersburg PA
CBHW020126180626
46810CB00004B/1427